W. S. Baker

American Engravers and Their Works

W. S. Baker

American Engravers and Their Works

ISBN/EAN: 9783337311223

Printed in Europe, USA, Canada, Australia, Japan

Cover: Foto ©Andreas Hilbeck / pixelio.de

More available books at **www.hansebooks.com**

AMERICAN ENGRAVERS

AND THEIR WORKS.

AMERICAN ENGRAVERS

AND

THEIR WORKS

BY

W. S. BAKER

Collige et inscribe

PHILADELPHIA

GEBBIE & BARRIE PUBLISHERS

1875

TO

GEORGE R. BONFIELD, Esq.,

In recognition of the

INTEREST TAKEN IN ITS PREPARATION,

THIS WORK

IS MOST SINCERELY INSCRIBED.

PREFACE.

————•————

A DESIRE on the part of the writer to ascertain what has been done by the plate engravers of America, led him, as time and opportunity served, to examine and note such of their productions as seemed either to be good examples of the artist, of moment historically, or interesting for the subject.

With accumulating material, there arose at the same time a wish to know something concerning the men with whose works he was becoming familiar, and the usual sources of information being found

extremely slight, he set himself about ob-
taining what was needed, either by actual
inquiry or through personal correspond-
ence.

Although not as complete as could be
wished, nor indeed as was intended—can a
work of this character ever be considered
complete?—the results of his labor are
now made public in the hope that the er-
rors and omissions may be charitably
viewed, since the purpose is simply to put
into a convenient form such facts as were
collected concerning our engravers and
their works, and thus be useful for future
reference.

While for this country, relatively speaking, we lay no claim to a national school
of Engraving, yet many admirable plates
have been produced, to which we can

point with reasonable pride, feeling that could the artistic talent, which since the first quarter of the century has been so completely engrossed in Bank Note work, have been otherwise directed, that our record would bear favorable comparison with the existing European schools.

In the department of Bank Note engraving, however, although much of its success is due to the ingenious application of mechanical contrivances, this country stands unrivalled. No such work has been produced elsewhere, and its gradual development from the rude essays of the early practitioners, to the almost perfect productions of the present day, forms not only a most interesting feature in the art, but furnishes also an instructive teaching of the wholesome influences of our form of government, which, when properly understood and administered, is sure to bring out all the energy, perseverance and talent of its citizens.

W. S. B.

Philadelphia,
Dec., 1875.

AMERICAN ENGRAVERS.

JOSEPH ANDREWS.

THIS admirable line engraver was born at Hingham, Mass., on the 17th day of August, 1806.

He showed an early inclination to art, and at fifteen years of age went to Boston, where he engaged with Abel Bowen, a wood engraver of that city. His first instructions in copper-plate engraving were, however, received from a certain Mr. Hoogland, who came to Boston in the year 1825. About the year 1827, he established himself with a brother (who was a printer) at Lancaster, Mass., in the engraving and printing business, his first plate from a painting and at the same time his first engraving on steel executed in 1829, being the small one after Alvan Fisher, entitled "The wicked flee where no man pursueth."

After producing other small plates for book publishers, he went in the year 1835 to London, where he studied for about nine months with Joseph Goodyear, under whose supervision he executed among others the small plate of "Annette de l' Arbre," after W. E. West. After visiting Paris with Mr. Goodyear, during which time he engraved the head of Benjamin Franklin, after a painting by Duplessis, now in the Public Library at Boston, he returned to America. In 1840, he again visited Europe, where he remained about two years, executing while in Paris six plates of portraits for the "Galerie Historique de Versailles," published under the auspices of Louis Philippe, one of them being Cardinal Tencin. In Florence, he commenced his plate of the "Duke of Urbino," after Titian, finished after his return home.

In 1855 he began his large work, "Plymouth Rock, 1620," after a painting by P. F. Rothermel, which was not finished until 1869.

Joseph Andrews died at Boston, May 7, 1873.

Earnest in the acquirement and prosecution of his art, his works are of that merit which entitle them to be classed among the best productions of the American burin. His head of Washington after Stuart, a peculiarly successful translation of the famous original, is admirably executed, while "Plymouth Rock, 1620," is a fine example of historical engraving.

WASHINGTON. Head and Bust. From the original painting by Stuart, in the Boston Athenæum. Small 4to. 1843.

BENJAMIN FRANKLIN. Head and Bust, the coat collar trimmed with fur. Duplessis, *Pinxt.* 4to.

OLIVER WOLCOTT. Head and Bust. After J. Trumbull. 8vo. 1846.

JOHN QUINCY ADAMS. Half Length Sitting, a book in his left hand. G. P. A. Healy, *Pinxt.* Folio. 1848.

Z. TAYLOR. Full Length, head only finished. Folio. 1848.

JARED SPARKS. After an unfinished picture by Gilbert Stuart. 8vo. 1855.

AMOS LAWRENCE. Three-quarter Length Sitting, head only finished. C. Harding, *Pinxt.* 8vo.

ABBOTT LAWRENCE. Head and Bust, the latter merely indicated. G. P. A. Healy, *Pinxt.* Engraved in 1849 in conjunction with T. Kelly. 8vo.

JAMES GRAHAM. Head and Bust. Healy, *Pinxt.* 8vo. 1845.

CHARLES SPRAGUE. Three-quarter Length Sitting, head only finished. 8vo. 1850.

THOMAS DOWSE. HALF LENGTH SITTING. M. WIGHT, *Pinxt.* 8vo. Private Plate.

DUKE OF URBINO. THREE-QUARTER LENGTH in armor. TITIAN, *Pinxt.* Folio.

PASSING THE FORD. ALVAN FISHER, *Pinxt.* 8vo. 1830.

THE PANTHER SCENE from "The Pioneers." GEO. L. BROWN, *Pinxt.* 8vo. 1835.

SWAPPING HORSES. W. S. MOUNT, *Pinxt.* 8vo. 1839.

PARSON WELLS AND HIS WIFE. F. O. C. Darley, *Delt.* 4to.

CHRISTIANA AND HER CHILDREN IN THE VALLEY OF DEATH. D. HUNTINGTON, *Pinxt.* Imp. Folio. *Mezzotinto.* Engraved in conjunction with C. E. Wagstaff. Art Union of Philadelphia, 1851.

THE WITCH OF ENDOR. WASH. ALLSTON, *Pinxt.* Ob. Roy. folio. *Mezzotinto.* In conjunction with C. E. Wagstaff.

THE PILGRIM'S PROGRESS. HAMMATT BILLINGS, *Delt.* Ob. Roy. folio. 1857.

PLYMOUTH ROCK 1620. PETER F. ROTHERMEL, *Pinxt.* Ob. Roy. folio. 1869.

W. G. ARMSTRONG,

LINE ENGRAVER, was born in Montgomery County, Penna., in 1823.

He was a pupil of James B. Longacre, and, while with him, engraved several heads for "The National Portrait Gallery," which are well executed.

He is a resident of Philadelphia, and has confined himself almost entirely to Bank Note work.

MAJOR GENERAL THOMAS PINCKNEY. Half Length in Uniform. J. Trumbull, *Pinxt.* 8vo.

MAJOR GENERAL WINFIELD SCOTT. Half Length Sitting, in Uniform, both hands (in Military Gloves) resting on his sword hilt. C. Ingham, *Pinxt.* 8vo.

JOHN McLANE. Half Length. T. Sully, *Pinxt.* 8vo.

HOPE. A Female Head of much character and expression. D. Huntington, *Pinxt.* 8vo. Executed in fine taste and ability.

E. S. BEST,

Line Engraver was born in London in 1826, and came to America about the year 1850.

He practiced in Philadelphia, and died in 1865. The following plates, particularly the one first mentioned, display superior technical ability.

GEORGE WASHINGTON AT VALLEY FORGE.
FULL LENGTH IN UNIFORM AND CLOAK, sitting at a table holding or rather clutching with a nervous grasp the celebrated "Duchè letter," the perusal of which has given an expression of deep thought to his countenance. C. SCHUSSELE, *Pinxt.* Roy. folio.

THE PARTING. G. E. SINTZENICH. Art Union of Philadelphia, 1853-4. Folio.

WILLIAM BIRCH,

Enamel Painter and Engraver, was born in Warwickshire, England, and coming to this country in 1794 settled in Philadelphia, where he died in 1834.

He designed and engraved quite a number of views of country seats in Pennsylvania and elsewhere, and others in the city of Philadelphia, besides those enumerated below. In the year 1800, with the

2

assistance of his son, Thomas Birch, well known afterwards as a Marine Painter, he published a series of folio plates entitled "The City of Philadelphia, in the State of Penna., North America, as it appeared in the year 1800, consisting of 28 Plates, drawn and engraved by W. Birch & Son."

With a Title Page and a general plan of the City; they are as follows:

FRONTISPIECE. The City and Port of Philadelphia on the River Delaware, from Kensington.

Arch Street Ferry.

Arch Street with the Second Presbyterian Church.

New Lutheran Church in Fourth Street.

Old Lutheran Church in Fifth Street.

South-East corner of Third and Market Streets.

High Street with the First Presbyterian Church.

High Street Market.

High Street from the Country Market Place with the procession in commemoration of the Death of General George Washington, Dec. 26, 1799.

High Street from Ninth Street.

The House intended for the President of the United States in Ninth St.

An unfinished House in Chestnut Street.

Second Street from Market St., with Christ Church.

New Market in South Second St.

Bank of the United States in Third Street.
View in Third Street from Spruce Street.
Library and Surgeons' Hall in Fifth Street.
Congress Hall and New Theatre in Chestnut Street.
State House with a view of Chestnut Street.
Back of the State House.
State House Garden.
Gaol in Walnut Street.
Alms House in Spruce Street.
Pennsylvania Hospital in Pine Street.
Bank of Pennsylvania, South Second Street.
The Water Works in Centre Square.
Preparation for War to defend Commerce. The Swedish
    Church Southwark with the building of the Frigate
    Philadelphia.
Bank of the United States with a view of Third St.

T. D. BOOTH.

OF this engraver no full particulars can be given. He is said to have been born in Albany, N. Y., and acquired the art in a Bank Note engraving establishment of that city, entering as a student somewhere about the year 1829.

During 1840–'42 he was working in New York City as an assistant to J. F. E. Prud'homme, and subsequently practiced in Cincinnati, which city he left about 1848, moving to Chicago and discontinuing engraving.

The following print, executed in line at Cincinnati, the only one bearing his name which has come under the notice of the compiler, is engraved in a broad, bold and effective manner, the production of a practiced hand.

THE TRAPPER'S LAST SHOT. W. RANNEY, *Pinxt.* " From the original painting distributed by the Western Art Union in 1850." Ob. Roy. folio.

J. BOYD.

AN Engraver in the stipple manner, who practiced in Philadelphia during the early part of the century.

FISHER AMES, Esq. HALF LENGTH SITTING, his left hand on an upright book, which rests on his knee. STUART, *Pinxt.* 8vo.

ELIAS BOUDINOT, LL. D. First Presd't of the Am Bible Soc. HEAD AND BUST IN ROBES. T. Sully, *Pinxt.* 8vo.

THE OLD ALMS HOUSE, on Spruce Street between 10th and 11th Streets, Philadelphia. Wm. Strickland, *Delt*. *Line*. Ob. large folio.

GEORGE L. BROWN,

Landscape Painter, was born in Boston, 1814.

Some attempts at scene painting while connected with a youthful dramatic club, exciting the admiration of his associates induced him to think of art as a profession, the first steps being made in the direction of wood engraving, soon to be abandoned, however, for the brush.

An early picture and the enthusiasm of the artist attracting the attention of a Boston merchant, funds were provided for a brief visit abroad for the purpose of study. Upon his return; a copy of one of Claude's Landscapes executed while in Europe, and declared by Washington Allston "to be

the best he ever saw," led others to interest themselves in advancing an artist of
such promise, and he was sent abroad for
a second time to fill a number of commis-
sions, and to properly prepare himself as
a painter.

During 1840–'46 he resided at Florence,
painting many admirable pictures, among
others a moonlight view of Venice, marked
for its beauty and truth of representation.

While at Rome, Mr. Brown executed,
1853–'55, a series of etchings (4to) nine in
number, published together in New York,
upon his return home in 1860, entitled
"Etchings of the Campagna, Rome." They
are neatly executed, and are as follows:

View of Palazzuolo, Lake Albano.
View of the road leading to Castello Gandolfo near
    Albano.
View at Ponto d'Arizio.
Cascade of Tivoli.
View near Rome.
View at Tivoli.

VIEW OF ARICCIA.
VIEW OF LAKE NEMI.
VIEW IN THE CAMPAGNA NEAR GENZANO.

CHARLES BURT.

THIS admirable line engraver was born at Edinburgh on the eighth day of Nov. 1822. At twelve years of age he entered with W. Home Lizars, engraver of that place, remaining with him until of age, during which time he was principally engaged on plates for Sir Wm. Jardine's Natural History. He shortly afterwards came to this country, and was employed by A. L. Dick, who, in his words, had an *establishment* for engraving in the city of New York, and with whom he remained for about four years. The admirable copy of Raphael Morghen's print of "The Last Supper" after Leonardo Da Vinci, which bears the name of A. L. Dick as engraver, was, according to his (Burt's) own statement executed entirely by himself, and occupied three years and nine months of the time he was with that engraver.

Since 1850 Mr. Burt has been engaged on Bank Note work, and for the last few years has been principal die engraver for the U. S. government.

His plates are carefully and ably engraved, good in character and drawing and accurate in detail. His Bank Note Portraits and Vignettes are choice examples of the art.

SIR WALTER RALEIGH PARTING WITH HIS WIFE. E. Leutze, *Pinxt.* Am. Art Union Print, 1846. Roy. folio.

THE SIGNING OF THE DEATH WARRANT OF LADY JANE GREY. D. Huntington, *Pinxt.* Am. Art Union Print, 1848. Ob. Roy. folio.

ANNE PAGE, SLENDER AND SHALLOW. C. R. Leslie, *Pinxt.* Am. Art Union Print, 1850. Ob. Roy. folio.

THE CARD PLAYERS. R. C. WOODVILLE, *Pinxt.*
   Am. Art Union Print, 1850. Ob. 4to.

MARION CROSSING THE PEDEE. W. RANNEY,
   Pinxt. Am. Art Union Print, 1851. Ob. 4to.

DUCK SHOOTING. W. RANNEY, *Pinxt.* Ob. 4to.

BARGAINING FOR A HORSE, W. S. MOUNT,
   Pinxt. Am. Art Union Print, 1851. Ob. 4to.

JOHN W. CASILEAR,

LANDSCAPE painter and engraver, was born
in the city of New York, June 1811. He
was originally a pupil of Peter Maverick
of that city, who, however, dying during the
time of his engagement, he finished his
term of study as an engraver with that admirable artist, Asher B. Durand.

In the direction of engraving his attention has been almost exclusively turned to
Bank Note work, to the artistic part of
which, he, as much as any other, has aided
in giving that superiority this department
has assumed in this country.

Since October, 1854, at which time he dissolved his connection with the Bank Note firm of Toppan, Carpenter, Casilear & Co., he has entirely devoted himself to landscape painting, visiting Europe during the years 1857–'58 for the purpose of study.

"His Bank Note designs have a light and graceful effect, and his engraving of Huntington's Sybil, published by the American Art Union, is a notable triumph of the burin; it has a sharpness and decision of line worthy of the celebrated old engravers." *Tuckerman.*

THE SEVEN PRESIDENTS.
George Washington, John Adams, Thomas Jefferson, James Madison, James Monroe, John Quincy Adams and Andrew Jackson. HEADS AND BUSTS in ornamental frames, grouped around a centre piece, in a folio sheet. ROBERT W. WEIR, *Delt.*

Painted and engraved expressly for the *New York Mirror.* Pub. 1834.

THE SIBYL. DANIEL HUNTINGTON, *Pinxt.* Am. Art. Union Print, 1847. Folio.

JOHN GADSBY CHAPMAN,

PAINTER and etcher, is a native of Alexandria, Va., born August 11th, 1808. He exhibited when quite young a decided talent for design, and studied and practiced his art in Italy for several years. Returning to America he opened a studio in the city of New York, where he was constantly employed in portrait painting, composition and illustrative designs. Since 1848 Mr. Chapman has resided in Rome. His etchings, original designs, are fine in character and drawing, and admirably executed.

THE RETURN FROM THE VINTAGE. A BEAUTIFUL GROUP of a peasant woman and children, two of whom are riding on a Donkey laden with grapes. Ob. oval 4to.

PIFERARI PLAYING BEFORE A SHRINE OF THE VIRGIN. FULL FIGURES. 4to. Roma, 1852.

A MONK SOLICITING ALMS. Full Figure. 4to. Roma, 1853.

ITALIAN GOAT HERDS. 4to. Roma, 1857.

THE GLEANER. An Italian Peasant Girl returning home. Full Figure. 4to. Roma, 1857.

A VIEW OF THE CAMPANA. Ob. oval 4to.

" Or where Campania's plain forsaken lies
A weary waste extending to the skies."

A VIEW IN THE VICINITY OF ROME. Ob. Oval 4to. Roma, 1852.

ON THE CAMPANA, WITH A DISTANT VIEW OF ST. PETER'S. Ob. oval 4to.

THE DEPARTURE OF SANCHO FOR THE GOVERNMENT OF HIS ISLAND. 8vo.

MASWADDOX CREEK, EASTERN SHORE, MARYLAND. Ob. 8vo.

HEAD OF REMBRANDT. After Rembrandt. 8vo.

HEAD OF RUBENS. 8vo. Florence, 1831.

THE AMBUSH WHEREBY AI WAS TAKEN. *Mezzotinto*. Ob. small 4to.

THE PLAGUE OF DARKNESS. *Mezzotinto*. Ob. small 4to.

JUDAS RECEIVING THE BRIBE. Half Length. *Mezzotinto*. 4to.

JOHN CHENEY,

THE best engraver of the female head in America, was born at Manchester, Conn., in the year 1801. When quite young, he showed much interest in engraving, and during his leisure hours while working on his father's farm, made some efforts in the art, without other instruction than that offered by books and the examination of such prints as came under his notice. For these essays he made his own tools, the plates being hammered out from the pieces of an old copper boiler.

When about twenty years of age he went to Hartford and worked with a Mr. Willard, a Map Engraver, and subsequently passed some time in Boston.

After studying several years in Europe, during which time he supported himself by his art, he returned to Boston and then went to Philadelphia, where he remained so long as he continued to engrave, relinquishing the practice of his profession when about fifty years of age.

His works, executed in line and principally heads, are all small; they are engraved in a peculiarly beautiful and artistic manner, and with the nicest taste, many being after Thomas Sully, for whose art he had the fullest sympathy.

MARTHA WASHINGTON. From the Head by Gilbert Stuart in the Boston Athenæum.

JOSEPH STORY, LL.D. HEAD AND BUST. W. W. STORY, *Delt.*

DANIEL WEBSTER. HALF LENGTH. From a miniature by R. M. STAIGG. Engraved in conjunction with R. W. Dodson.

EDWARD EVERETT. HEAD AND BUST. From a miniature by R. M. STAIGG.

FRANCES ANNE KEMBLE. HEAD AND BUST, showing the back and shoulders, which are partly undraped. THOS. SULLY, *Pinxt.*

EDITH MAY. Nom-de-plume of Miss Anne Drinker,

Poetess. HEAD AND BUST. W. H. FURNESS, Jr., *Pinxt.*

MERCY'S DREAM. DANIEL HUNTINGTON, *Pinxt.*

A FLORENTINE GIRL. HALF LENGTH. DANIEL HUNTINGTON, *Pinxt.*

MAIDENHOOD. THREE-QUARTER LENGTH STANDING. DANIEL HUNTINGTON, *Pinxt.* Engraved in conjunction with J. I. PEASE.

PRECIOSA. THREE-QUARTER LENGTH SITTING. DANIEL HUNTINGTON, *Pinxt.*

THE ROMAN GIRL. HALF LENGTH, carrying on her head a water jar, with the usual head-dress of the country. DANIEL HUNTINGTON, *Pinxt.*

THE LOVE LETTER. A reclining female figure. T. SULLY, *Pinxt.*

PORTRAIT OF A LADY, shading her eyes with a fan. T. SULLY, *Pinxt.*

FEMALE HEAD, showing back and shoulders. T. SULLY, *Pinxt.*

ISABELLA. HALF LENGTH, attired as a novice. T. SULLY, *Pinxt.*

THE GIPSY. A reclining position, the head and shoulders only visible. T. SULLY, *Pinxt.*

THE COUNTRY GIRL. HALF LENGTH STANDING, holding with the left hand a basket which rests partly on a wall. T. SULLY, *Pinxt*

CHILDHOOD. Portrait of a boy nude to the middle. T. SULLY, *Pinxt.*

DULCINEA. Three-quarter Figure, sitting arranging her hair. C. R. Leslie, *Pinxt.*

BEATRICE. Half Figure Sitting. Wash. Allston, *Pinxt.*

INCOGNITA. Head and Shoulders, turned to the left. S. W. Cheney, *Delt.*

VIOLA. Head and Shoulders of a young girl, turned to the right. S. W. Cheney, *Delt.*

A FEMALE HEAD ADORNED WITH A TURBAN. Portrait of Mrs. Blodgett. G. Stuart, *Pinxt.*

ANNETTE. Head and Bust of a young girl, the hair short and loose over the forehead. From a miniature by E. Malbone.

EGERIA. A Head of Much Beauty. From a miniature by E. Malbone.

A FEMALE HEAD OF THE MOORISH TYPE. A veil over the head and shoulders. E. Leutze, *Delt.*

GUARDIAN ANGELS. Sir Joshua Reynolds, *Pinxt.*

CEPHAS G. CHILDS,

Line engraver, was born in Bucks County, Penna., on the eighth day of September, 1793, and died at Philadelphia, July 7, 1871.

When about fourteen years of age, he went as an apprentice to Gideon Fairman, Engraver of Philadelphia, with whom he afterwards formed business relations. In 1831, he made a short visit to Europe, and upon his return entered into partnership with the late Henry Inman, Portrait Painter, in the Lithographic printing and publishing business, having in their employ Albert Neusam, deceased, a deaf mute of considerable talent and a most excellent draughtsman of the head.

The connection with Inman was dissolved about the year 1835, Mr. Childs then becoming identified as the publisher of a mercantile paper, "The Commercial List."

In the years 1827 to 1830, he published a set of 8vo. views in Philadelphia and its vicinity, engraved with but few exceptions by himself, all of which are well executed.

3

The following are those engraved by Mr. Childs:

SWEDISH LUTHERAN CHURCH.   T. SULLY, *Delt.*
WATER WORKS.   T. Doughty, *Pinxt.*
VIEW ON THE SCHUYLKILL FROM THE OLD WATER WORKS.
                                Captain J. R. Watson, *Delt.*
SEDGELEY PARK.   E. W. Clay, *Delt.*
PENNSYLVANIA INSTITUTION FOR THE DEAF AND DUMB.
                                Geo. Strickland, *Delt.*
STATE HOUSE OR HALL OF INDEPENDENCE. "   "   "
BANK OF THE UNITED STATES.   "   "   "
PENNSYLVANIA HOSPITAL.   "   "   "
PENNSYLVANIA ACADEMY OF THE FINE
      ARTS.   "   "   "
CHRIST CHURCH.   "   "   "
SAINT STEPHEN'S CHURCH.   "   "   "
GIRARD'S BANK, LATE UNITED STATES
      BANK.   "   "   "
ACADEMY OF NATURAL SCIENCES.   "   "   "
FIRST CONGREGATIONAL UNITARIAN CHURCH.
                                H. Reinagle, *Delt.*
EASTERN PENITENTIARY OF PENNSYLVANIA, W. Mason,   "
EAGLESFIELD,   "   "   "
SCHUYLKILL CANAL AT MANAYUNK.   Geo. Lehman,   "

JOHN CHORLEY.

THE name "John Chorley, Boston," appears on the following copy of James

Heath's print after Stuart's full length Washington, known as the "Lansdowne Portrait." It is executed in line and very well engraved.

No other production of this engraver has come under the notice of the Compiler.

GENERAL WASHINGTON. Full Length Standing, the right arm extended, the left hand on his sword. G. Stuart, *Pinxt.* 1797. Roy. folio.

J. CONE,

Line engraver, who practiced the art in Philadelphia, in the early part of the century.

The following prints engraved for Childs' views in that city published in 1828, are well executed. The first mentioned being the Frontispiece to that work.

PHILADELPHIA FROM KENSINGTON. T. Birch, *Delt.* 8vo.

FAIRMOUNT WATER WORKS FROM THE WEST BANK OF THE SCHUYLKILL. T. DOUGHTY, *Delt.* 8vo.

GEORGE H. CUSHMAN,

LINE ENGRAVER, was born at Plainfield, Conn., about 1814, and acquired the art in Boston, studying drawing under Washington Allston.

In 1835, he went to Philadelphia, where he practiced for many years, working in the same studio with that admirable engraver, John Cheney.

Since 1860, when he moved to New York City, Mr. Cushman has (until quite recently) done but little engraving, turning his attention to miniature painting, in which he has been particularly successful, producing some exquisite examples of the art.

His works, Book Plates, comprising Portraits, Subjects and Landscapes, are executed with much taste and ability.

M. I. DANFORTH.

THIS admirable line engraver was born in Hartford, Conn., and in 1818 began the art as a pupil of "The Graphic Company" of that place, an association for the purpose of executing Bank Note plates.

In 1821, he moved to New Haven and commenced engraving on his own account, during which period he executed for a publisher of Hartford, a copy of Raphael Morghen's print after Titian, "Parce Somnum Rumpere," of the same size, and most admirably done. In 1826, he went to New York and studied in the school of the National Academy of Design, and the following year went to London, where he remained some time studying and perfecting himself in his art. Upon his return home he entered with others into the

Bank Note engraving business in New York City. He died about fifteen years ago.

His "Sentry Box" after C. R. Leslie, engraved in London, in 1832, is a fine example of line engraving.

WASHINGTON IRVING. HEAD AND FULL BUST, the coat collar trimmed with fur. C. R. LESLIE, *Pinxt*. Pub. in London, 1831. 4to.

SIR WALTER SCOTT. HALF LENGTH SITTING, a cane in his right hand, while the left holds a Scotch cap or bonnet. C. R. LESLIE, *Pinxt*. 8vo.

THE SENTRY BOX. UNCLE TOBY AND THE WIDOW WADMAN. C. R. LESLIE, *Pinxt*. London, 1832. Folio.

DON QUIXOTE. FULL BUST. C. R. LESLIE, *Pinxt*. 8vo.

PARCE SOMNUM RUMPERE. Titian, *Pinxt*. Ob. folio.

FELIX O. C. DARLEY.

THIS admirable designer was born at Philadelphia, June 23, 1822. Placed by his parents at the age of fourteen in a

Mercantile House, he devoted his leisure hours to drawing, and receiving a handsome sum for some designs, applied himself wholly to the art, and was soon fully employed by the large publication houses of his native city.

In 1848, he moved to New York, where he illustrated the "Sketch Book," "Knickerbocker," &c. His designs for Bank Note Vignettes, and the Illustrations to Cooper's Works, Irving's Washington and Dickens' Works are well known and highly esteemed. They are most beautifully and artistically composed, and replete with character and interest, and as illustrations are almost unequalled.

He designed and etched in outline on stone (oblong folio), for Irving's "Rip Van Winkle" and "The Legend of Sleepy Hollow," twelve (six each) characteristic and humorous illustrations.

Rip Van Winkle.

Rip Van Winkle's Wife on Washing Day.
Rip Amusing the Children of the Village.
Rip and the Village Club before the Small Inn.
Rip Waiting upon the Nine Pin Players in the Kaatskill Mts.
Rip as an Old Man before the door of his dilapidated House.
Rip telling his Story in front of " The Union Hotel."

The Legend of Sleepy Hollow.

Ichabod Crane in the School Room.
Ichabod Reciting Witchcraft Stories of a Winter Evening.
Ichabod and Katrina Van Tassel under the Great Elm.
Ichabod and Katrina dancing at the Quilting Party.
Ichabod meeting the Headless Horseman of Sleepy Hollow.
Ichabod attempting to escape from the Headless Horseman.

A. L. DICK,

LINE ENGRAVER, was a Scotchman by birth,
and acquired the art under Robert Scott
of Edinburgh, previously to coming to
America, 1833. He carried on the business of engraving quite extensively in the
City of New York, taking pupils and em-
ploying assistants.

His name appears on numerous Book

Plates for Annuals, Magazines and the like. He died in 1865, at the age of sixty.

THE LAST SUPPER. Leonardo da Vinci, *Pinxt.*
   Ob. Imp. folio.
A very excellent copy of the Raphael Morghen Print, and of the same size.

SCHUYLKILL WATER WORKS. W. H. Bart-
   lett. Ob. 4to.

RICHARD W. DODSON.

This excellent line engraver was born at Cambridge, Maryland, on the Fifth day of February, 1812, and died at Cape May, N. J., July 23, 1867.

When about sixteen years of age, he entered with James B. Longacre, of Philadelphia, to acquire the art, remaining with him until twenty-one years of age.

He practiced in that city until 1845, at which time he entirely discontinued engraving.

His plates, all small, are executed with

much taste and ability; the portrait of Philip Syng Physick, M. D., after H. Inman, is a choice example of the art.

BENJAMIN FRANKLIN. HALF LENGTH, wearing a coat trimmed with fur. From a miniature.

GENERAL JONATHAN WILLIAMS. THREE QUARTER LENGTH SITTING. T. SULLY, *Pinxt.*

RICHARD DALE, COMMANDER U.S.N. HEAD AND FULL BUST in uniform. J. WOOD, *Pinxt.*

MAJOR GEN. WILLIAM HENRY HARRISON. HALF LENGTH. J. R. LAMBDIN, *Pinxt.*

SIMON KENTON. (Kentucky Pioneer.) HALF LENGTH SITTING with a staff in his right hand. L. W. MORGAN, *Pinxt.*

BENJAMIN RUSH, M.D. THREE QUARTER LENGTH sitting at a Table, on which lies an open Book, the fingers of his right hand between the leaves. T. SULLY, *Pinxt.*

PHILIP SYNG PHYSICK, M.D. THREE QUARTER LENGTH sitting in an arm-chair at a Table; to the right between some pillars a view of a distant landscape. H. Inman, *Pinxt.*

DANIEL WEBSTER. HEAD AND FULL BUST. From a miniature by R. M. STAIGG. Engraved in conjunction with John CHENEY.

HENRY D. GILPIN. Atty. Gen. U. S. HEAD AND FULL BUST. H. INMAN, *Pinxt.*

RIGHT REV. WILLIAM WHITE, D. D. BISHOP OF PENNA. HEAD AND BUST. H. INMAN, *Pinxt.*

RIGHT REV. RICHARD CHANNING MOORE, D. D. HALF LENGTH in robes, right hand resting on an upright Book. H. INMAN, *Pinxt.*

RIGHT REV. ALEXANDER V. GRISWOLD, D. D. HEAD AND BUST in robes. H. INMAN, *Pinxt.*

CHARLES WILKES, COMMANDER U. S. N. HEAD AND FULL BUST. T. SULLY, *Pinxt.* 4to.

SIR WALTER SCOTT, BART. FULL FIGURE sitting among some ruins by moonlight. SIR H. RAEBURN, *Pinxt.*

WASHINGTON AND GIST CROSSING THE ALLEGHANY ON A RAFT (1753). D. HUNTINGTON, *Pinxt.*

THE NEWS BOY. FULL FIGURE. H. INMAN, *Pinxt.*

THE LACE CAP. PORTRAIT OF A YOUTHFUL MATRON in cap and short curls. T. SULLY, *Pinxt.* Engraved in conjunction with JOHN CHENEY.

MIRANDA. HALF LENGTH, with hands clasped in front, the arms resting on some rocks. T. SULLY, *Pinxt.*

"OF SUCH IS THE KINGDOM OF HEAVEN." A child fondling a bird. THREE QUARTER FIGURE. M. I. De FRANCA, *Pinxt.*

AMOS DOOLITTLE.

THIS early practitioner of the art was born at Cheshire, Conn., and died at New

Haven the Thirty-first day of January, 1832, aged seventy-eight years. He was brought up as a silversmith, and at twenty-one commenced business as an engraver, in which he was self-taught.

While a volunteer at Cambridge, he visited the battle-ground at Lexington, and on his return to New Haven made an engraving of the action, his first attempt at an historical plate. He also executed three other historical prints in relation to the expedition to Lexington and Concord, all from drawings made on the spot by Mr. Earl, a portrait painter.

THE BATTLE OF LEXINGTON.

A VIEW OF THE TOWN OF CONCORD WITH THE MINISTERIAL TROOPS DESTROYING THE STORES.

THE BATTLE OF THE NORTH BRIDGE IN CONCORD.

THE SOUTH PART OF LEXINGTON WHEN THE FIRST DETACHMENT WAS JOINED BY LORD PERCY.

THE BATTLE OF LEXINGTON. A reduced copy of the first, for Barber's History of New Haven, executed in 1832.

GEN. GEORGE WASHINGTON, COMMANDER-IN-CHIEF OF THE UNITED STATES. Born Feb'y. 11, 1732, O. S., died December 14, 1799. PROFILE HEAD AND BUST from a Medallion. Over the head an eagle holding a wreath. Small 8vo. STIPPLE.

ASHER BROWN DURAND.

THIS admirable painter and distinguished line engraver was born (of Huguenot ancestry,) at Jefferson Village, now South Orange, New Jersey, on the 21st day of August, 1796.

In the shop of his father, who was a watch-maker, he learned to cut cyphers on spoons, and early in life showed a disposition to acquire the elements of the art in which he has since become so eminent. His first attempts at engraving for the purpose of taking impressions therefrom (induced by the perusal of a work treating on the art,) were made on plates hammered out from copper coins, the tools being manufactured by himself, his models being the circular cards which it was then the custom to insert in watch-cases.

A French gentleman, struck with the talent which some of these evinced, employed him to copy a portrait painted on the lid of a snuff-box, and the success with which this commission was executed encouraged him to make engraving his profession.

In 1812 he became an apprentice to Peter Maverick, of New York, a prominent Engraver at the time, and with whom, after becoming of age (1817,) he entered into business relations, which, however, lasted but a few years.

His first important production was the large Plate of the "Declaration of Independence," after Trumbull's well-known picture, published in 1820, upon which he worked some three years, and which establishing his reputation as a first-class engraver, led to constant employment.

After fifteen years of prosperous labor in his profession he was induced to abandon it for portrait and landscape painting, in the latter of which he has achieved such distinguished success as to place him in the front rank of American Painters.

His last work was the "Ariadne," after Vanderlyn, published in 1835, a fit closing of his career as an Engraver.

A. B. Durand is the acknowledged head of the profession in America. A fine draughtsman, and with thorough command of the burin, his plates are executed in the finest feeling and the most artistic manner.

In the rendering of flesh he was particularly successful; the "Ariadne" is not alone the finest example of the nude yet produced in this country, but it is as a whole a most admirable work of art, every portion of it most delicately and beautifully engraved, every detail most truthfully and agreeably given.   Contemporary European art furnishes no better specimen of the higher walks of the profession.

The "Musidora," his own design, is a chaste and beautiful realization of the Poet's lines,

> " ——With timid eye, around
> The banks surveying, stripp'd her beauteous limbs
> To taste the lucid coolness of the flood."

His portraits are truthful in character and expression, and admirably executed. That of Charles Carroll, after Chester Harding, engraved for "The National Portrait Gallery," excited much surprise abroad at the time of its publication, as being the work of an American.

. D urand was Recording Secretary

of the National Academy of Design for six years, Vice President for the year 1844, and in the following year President, which office he held for sixteen years, declining a re-election in favor of Prof. Morse.

He resides at his native place, and now in the eightieth year of his age, is still practicing painting, having just finished a large Landscape representing a view of Lake George.

GEORGE WASHINGTON. HALF LENGTH IN UNIFORM. From the full length by Col. Trumbull. Frontispiece to the 1st Vol. of "The Nat. Port. Gallery." 8vo.

GEORGE WASHINGTON. HEAD AND BUST. G. STUART, *Pinxt.* 8vo.

JAMES MONROE. HALF LENGTH. J. Vanderlyn, *Pinxt.* 8vo.

JOHN QUINCY ADAMS, President of the United States. FULL LENGTH, sitting near a table in a library holding in both hands an open folio volume. T. Sully, *Pinxt.* Published Oct. 6, 1826, by W. H. Morgan, 114 Chesnut St., Philada. Roy. folio.

CHARLES CARROLL OF CARROLLTON. HEAD AND FULL BUST. C. Harding, *Pinxt.* 8vo.

JOHN JAY, 1st Chief Justice of the U. S. Nearly Full Length, Sitting, his right arm resting on a table upon which are some books. Stuart & Trumbull, *Pinxt.* 8vo.

JAMES KENT, LL.D. Half Length Sitting. F. R. Spencer, *Pinxt.* 8vo.

JOHN MARSHALL, LL.D. Nearly Three-quarter Length Sitting, his right hand resting upon an upright book. Henry Inman, *Pinxt.* 8vo.

JUDGE PLATT. Head and Bust. J. Trumbull, *Pinxt.* 4to.

JOHN TRUMBULL. Half Length. Waldo & Jewett, *Pinxt.* 8vo.

GILBERT CHARLES STUART. Head and full Bust. From a miniature by Sarah Goodrich. 8vo.

De WITT CLINTON. Half Length Sitting. C. Ingham, *Pinxt.* 8vo.

AARON OGDEN. Head and Bust, on the left breast the order of the Cincinnati. A. B. Durand, *Pinxt.* 8vo.

OLIVER WOLCOTT. Governor of Connecticut. Head and Bust. Thos. Sully, *Pinxt.* 4to.

JOEL BARLOW. (Author of the Columbiad). Nearly Three-quarter Length Sitting, holding a manuscript in his right hand. Robert Fulton, *Pinxt.* 8vo.

STEPHEN DECATUR. Three quarter Length Standing, figure in profile, right hand resting on his sword hilt. T. Sully, *Pinxt.* 8vo.

GENERAL ANDREW JACKSON, New Orleans,

Jany. 8, 1815. FULL LENGTH STANDING, in uniform, pointing with his sword to the battle, which is raging in the right distance. Immediately in the rear of his figure is a horse fully caparisoned, held by a soldier. JOHN VANDERLYN, *Pinxt.* Pub. at New York, June 1828. Roy. folio.

WILLIAM H. CRAWFORD. HEAD AND FULL BUST. J. W. JARVIS, *Pinxt.* 4to.

REV. WILLIAM JAY. HEAD AND FULL BUST in robes, eye-glasses in his right hand. BRANWHITE, *Delt.* 4to.

VALENTINE MOTT, D. D. HEAD AND FULL BUST. H. INMAN, *Pinxt.* 8vo.

REV. JOHN MASON. JARVIS, *Pinxt.* Roy. 4to.

REV. ELIAS BOUDINOT, LL.D. THREE-QUARTER LENGTH SITTING. WALDO & JEWETT, *Pinxt.* Roy. 4to.

REV. ELIPHALET NOTT. HEAD AND BUST. AMES, *Pinxt.* 8vo.

REV. W. B. SPRAGUE. HEAD AND BUST. S. F. B. MORSE, *Pinxt.* 8vo.

REV. JOHN SUMMERFIELD. HEAD AND BUST. WALDO & JEWETT, *Pinxt.* Roy. 8vo.

DAVID HOSACK, M. D., F. R. S. THREE-QUARTER LENGTH, sitting at a table, his right hand resting upon an upright Book. T. SULLY, *Pinxt.* 8vo.

WILLIAM SWAIM. HEAD AND FULL BUST. INMAN, *Delt.* 4to.

PHILIP HONE. R. PEALE, *Pinxt.* 4to.

WILLIAM PAULDING.　A. B. DURAND, *Delt.*　4to.

DAVID CROCKETT.　HEAD AND BUST.　DE ROSE, *Pinxt.*　4to.

JAMES H. HACKETT.　HEAD AND BUST.　H. INMAN, *Pinxt.*　8vo.

FULLER THE GYMNAST.　FULL LENGTH STANDING in the act of boxing.　INGHAM, *Pinxt.*　Roy. folio.

DECLARATION OF INDEPENDENCE.　J. TRUMBULL, Esq., *Pinxt.*　Pub. 1820.　Ob. Extra Imp. folio. "It represents the Congress at the moment when the Committee, who drew up the Declaration advanced to the Table of the President to make their report."

MUSIDORA.　THOMSON'S SEASONS.　FULL FIGURE, Designed and engraved by A. B. DURAND, New York. 1825.　Folio.

ARIADNE.　FULL FIGURE, reclining, asleep.　JOHN VANDERLYN, *Pinxt.*　Pub. 1835.　Ob. Roy. folio.

DELAWARE WATER GAP.　A. B. DURAND, *Delt.*　Ob. 4to.

WINNIPISEOGEE LAKE.　T. COLE, *Pinxt.*　Ob. 4to.

FORT PUTNAM.　ROBT. W. WEIR, *Pinxt.*　Ob. 4to.

WEEHAWKEN.　W. J. BARRETT.　Ob. 4to.

CATSKILL MOUNTAINS.　A. B. DURAND, *Delt.*　Ob. 4to.

DAVID EDWIN.

THIS excellent engraver, in the Stipple manner, the son of John Edwin, a celebrated comedian of the day, was born at Bath, England, December, 1776. He was articled to Jossi, a Dutch engraver at that time practicing in England, and who returned to Holland in the year 1796, taking his apprentice, then twenty years of age, with him.

After arriving at Amsterdam the instructor and pupil did not agree, and before the term of apprenticeship had expired, they separated, young Edwin at one and twenty years of age finding himself in a foreign country, without friends or money. There being no direct communication with England at that time, Edwin, in his anxiety to leave, and in the hope of ultimately reaching London, entered himself under the American flag, in a ship bound for Philadelphia, to work his passage as a sailor before the mast. He landed in that city in the month of December, 1797, after being nearly five months on shipboard.

Having heard that his countryman, T. B. Freeman, resided in Philadelphia and carried on business as a publisher, he waited upon him, stated his name, circumstances and profession, and solicited employment. He was well received, and employed to engrave a title page to a collection of Scotch airs selected by Benjamin Carr, which Mr. Freeman was about publishing.

He experienced much difficulty in executing this work, both from want of the necessary tools and the rude finish of the plate, added to which was the lack of a proper press, it being almost impossible to take off a tolerable impression from the one then in use by the principal printer in Philadelphia. But our young artist overcame all these disadvantages, and produced a satisfactory print.

He devoted himself entirely to portrait engraving, in which he was eminently successful, and was termed "The first good engraver of the human countenance that appeared in this country." His plates, executed in a broad, effective and artistic manner, show good drawing, and are faithful renderings of the originals. Those after Stuart, of whose friendship he was exceedingly proud, are admirable translations of the breadth of handling and peculiar qualities of that eminent portrait painter. He died at Philadelphia, February 22, 1841.

GEORGE WASHINGTON. Head and full Bust. G. Stuart, *Pinxt.* 4to.

GEN. GEO. WASHINGTON. Born Feb. 22, 1732, in Westmoreland County, Virginia, and died Dec.

14, 1779, AT MT. VERNON. HEAD AND FULL BUST.
R. PEALE, *Pinxt.* Large 4to.

HIS EXCELLENCY, GEORGE WASHINGTON,
LIEUT. GENL. OF THE ARMIES OF THE U. S. OF AM.
Half length sitting in uniform and tie wig. In his right
hand a chart, while his sword rests on the fore-arm; on
the left breast the order of the Cincinnati. F. BARTOLI,
Pinxt. Pub. by D. Kennedy, No. 228 Market St.,
Philad'a. 4to.

APOTHEOSIS OF WASHINGTON. Full figure
sitting on clouds, a cherub in the act of crowning him
with a wreath; beneath a view of Mt. Vernon. R.
PEALE, *Pinxt.* Pub. by S. Kennedy, No. 129 Chesnut
St., corner of 4th, Philad'a. Royal folio.

**JAMES MADISON, President of the United
States of America.** HALF LENGTH SITTING, show-
ing right hand. STEWART, *Pinxt.* Folio. Baltimore.
Published Jany. 1809, by C. BOYLE.

**JAMES MADISON, President of the United
States.** FULL LENGTH, STANDING near a table on
which lies a paper partly rolled, entitled "Constitution of
the United States." STUART & SULLY, *Pinxt.* Pub.
March 1, 1810, by W. H. Morgan & Co., Philad'a. Folio.

MRS. MADISON. HALF LENGTH SITTING, full dress,
low neck and bare arms. G. STUART, *Pinxt.* 4to.

**THOMAS JEFFERSON, ESQ., Vice President
of the United States.** HEAD AND FULL BUST.
R. PEALE, *Pinxt.* Pub. by B. Savage, 1800. Large 4to.

GENERAL KNOX. HEAD AND FULL BUST. C. W.
PEALE, *Pinxt.* Oval, 8vo.

GEN. D. MORGAN. HEAD AND BUST IN UNIFORM. C. W. PEALE, *Pinxt.* 8vo.

STEPHEN DECATUR, ESQ., of the U. S. Navy. HEAD AND FULL BUST in uniform. G. STUART, *Pinxt.* 8vo.

ISAAC HULL, ESQ., of the U. S. Navy. HEAD AND FULL BUST in uniform. G. STUART, *Pinxt.* 8vo.

JACOB JONES, of the U. S. Navy. HEAD AND FULL BUST in uniform. REMBRANDT PEALE, *Pinxt.* 8vo.

JAMES LAWRENCE, ESQ., Late of the U. S. Navy. HEAD AND FULL BUST in uniform. G. STUART, *Pinxt.* 8vo.

OLIVER H. PERRY, ESQ., Late of the U. S. Navy. HEAD AND FULL BUST in uniform. WALDO, *Pinxt.* 8vo.

DAVID PORTER, ESQ., of the U. S. Navy. HEAD AND FULL BUST in uniform, left hand and arm introduced. WOOD, *Pinxt.* 8vo.

RICHARD DALE, ESQ., Late of the U. S. Navy. HEAD AND FULL BUST. WOOD, *Pinxt.* 8vo.

JOHN RODGERS, ESQ., of the U. S. Navy. HEAD AND FULL BUST in uniform. JARVIS, *Pinxt.* 8vo.

WILLIAM BAINBRIDGE, of the U. S. N. HEAD AND FULL BUST in uniform. G. STUART, *Pinxt.* 8vo.

MAJOR GENL. WINFIELD SCOTT, of the U. S. Army. HEAD AND FULL BUST in uniform. WOOD, *Pinxt.* 8vo.

THOMAS McKEAN, Governor of the Common-wealth of Penna.; Vice-Presdt. of the State Society of Cincinnati. HEAD AND FULL BUST, tie wig. On the left breast the order of the Cincinnati. GILBERT STUART, *Pinxt.*

Pub. Jany. 14, 1803, by Stuart & Edwin. 4to.

SIMON SNYDER, Governor of the State of Penna. HALF LENGTH SITTING, a roll of paper in his right hand which rests upon a table. T. SULLY, *Pinxt.* Large 4to.

"Dedicated to the people of Penna. by their Fellow Citizen, John Binns." Pub. Philada., July, 1809.

EDWARD SHIPPEN, L L. D., CHIEF JUSTICE OF PENNA.; Ætat. 74. HEAD AND FULL BUST. G. STUART, *Pinxt.* 8vo.

ALEXANDER WILSON. HEAD AND BUST. PEALE, *Pinxt.* 8vo. oval.

WILLIAM SMITH, D. D. Ætat. 75. First Provost of the University of Penna. HEAD AND FULL BUST IN ROBES. G. STUART, *Pinxt.* 8vo.

JOHN ANDREWS, D. D., Provost of the University of Penna. HEAD AND FULL BUST IN ROBES. T. SULLY, *Pinxt.* 8vo. oval.

THE RIGHT REV. WILLIAM WHITE, D. D., Bishop of the Protestant Episcopal Church in the State of Penna. HEAD AND FULL BUST IN ROBES. 8vo. oval.

GILBERT STUART. Ætat. 72. HEAD AND FULL BUST. JOHN NEAGLE, *Pinxt.* 8vo.

BENJAMIN RUSH, M. D. THREE QUARTER LENGTH, sitting at a table, his right hand resting upon an open Book. T. SULLY, *Pinxt.* 8vo. Pub. 1813.

PETER FRANCISCUS' gallant action with nine of Tarleton's Cavalry in sight of a troop of 400 men. (Amelia County, Virginia, 1781). JAS. WARREL, *Delt.* Pub. Dec. 1, 1814, by James Webster of Philad'a. Ob. Imp. folio.

GEORGE B. ELLIS,

LINE ENGRAVER, of whom no information could be obtained. He seems to have worked entirely for Book Publishers. The following annual Prints are well engraved.

DELAWARE WATER GAP. T. DOUGHTY, *Pinxt.* 8vo.
LAKE SCENE. " " "
CATSKILL FALLS. " " "

GIDEON FAIRMAN,

A CAPTAIN and then a colonel of militia and volunteers in the war of 1812, was born at Newtown, Fairfield County, Conn., on the twenty-sixth day of June, 1774, and at an early age exhibited considerable mechanical ingenuity and a taste for the fine arts.

The family becoming reduced in circumstances, he placed himself as an apprentice to a certain Isaac Crane, a blacksmith of New Mitford, a short distance from his native place. While thus employed some rude specimens of engraving made with tools of his own construction, attracted the attention of an English engraver by the name of Brunton, who advised him to follow a pursuit for which he displayed such a strong proclivity.

He accordingly, when about eighteen years of age, determined to leave a place where he could obtain no instruction in the art, and started on foot with a very limited supply of money (eighteen cents,) and walked to Hudson, on the North River. From thence he found means to reach Albany, where he bound himself as an apprentice to Isaac & George Hutton, Jewelers and Engravers, with whom he remained until of age, steadily improving under the limited advantages given him by his employers.

In 1796 he commenced business for himself, winning the good opinion of all by a natural grace of manner, and a steady application to business. In 1810 he went to Philadelphia, and in the following year became associated with George Murray and others, in the Bank note engraving business, under the firm name of Murray, Draper, Fairman & Co., afterwards so widely known in this branch of the art. In 1814 they associated with them Jacob Perkins, who had previously substituted steel for copper plates and invented the transferring process (vide Jacob Perkins,) and from that time, Asa Spencer also connected with them, having shortly afterwards succeeded in applying lathe work to the die plate, may be dated the revolution in this department of the art which has raised Bank Note engraving to a specialty, and in which the artists and mechanics of the United States have nearly attained perfection.

In the year 1818 Mr. Fairman, accompanied by Jacob Perkins, Asa Spencer, and a number of workmen, went to London to compete for the premium of £20,000, offered by the Bank of England for a plate which could not be counterfeited, which they claimed for their work. But an English Engraver, having succeeded after many efforts in closely imitating the lathe work, they withdrew from the contest, all, with the exception of Jacob Perkins, returning to this country.

The Directors of the Bank, however, awarded them £5,000, in consideration of their ingenuity and enterprise, at the same time fully recognizing the great merit of their inventions and applications.

Gideon Fairman died April 18, 1827. He was an excellent designer and draughtsman, and his small figures for Bank Note Vignettes were executed with much taste and ability.

GEO. WASHINGTON. HEAD AND FULL BUST. G. STUART, *Pinxt.* Up. oval. 8vo. *Stipple.*

GEO. WASHINGTON. HEAD AND FULL BUST. G. STUART, *Pinxt.* 4to. *Stipple.*

WILLIAM MOULTRIE, Esq. HEAD AND BUST in uniform. C. FRASER, *Pinxt.* Oval 8vo. *Stipple.*

STEPHEN J. FERRIS,

PORTRAIT and figure painter, was born near Plattsburg, N. Y., on the twenty-fifth day of January, 1835.

Although showing from early childhood a taste and inclination for drawing, it was

not until he was twenty-one years of age
that it took such shape as to apply himself
to really acquire a knowledge of art.   He
then, the previous twelve years of his life
having been passed in the State of Illinois,
went to Philadelphia (where he has since
resided), and entered the studio of the
well-known portrait painter, S. B. Waugh,
with whom he remained for two years,
studying portraiture and paying close attention to figure drawing.

Many of his portraits are in crayon, and
held in much esteem.   Mr. Ferris has
lately taken up the acid and needle, and
has etched several plates with good success, that of the "Chariot Race in the
Circus Maximus" being the most important.

GEORGE WASHINGTON. From Stuart's Head in the
    Boston Athenæum.   Folio.

MARIANO FORTUNY. Half Length.   4to.

CHARIOT RACE in the Circus Maximus at Rome in the presence of the Emperor Domitian. A. WAGNER, *Pinxt.* Etched in conjunction with Peter Moran. Ob. Roy. folio.

THE FARMER'S BOY. From a study by L. KNAUS. 4to.

THE TURNIP BOY. From a study by L. KNAUS. 4to.

R. FIELD,

MINIATURE painter and engraver, was an Englishman by birth. He practiced in Boston, Philadelphia and Baltimore, about the end of the last and the commencement of the present century, and from the United States went to Halifax.

He was a good painter and an excellent engraver in the stipple manner.

GEORGE WASHINGTON, Presdt. of the U. S. HEAD AND FULL BUST in uniform. Oval 8vo. in an ornamented scroll frame. On the point of a sword which extends from the top of the frame is a liberty cap, and around the blade a wreath across which is the word " Libertas." Below the frame an eagle with a scroll and the motto " E. Pluribus unum." Jos.

J. Barralett, Invenit. 1795. W. Robertson, *Pinxt.*
Pub. 1st Aug. 1795. Folio plate.

THOMAS JEFFERSON. Head and full Bust. G.
Stuart, *Pinxt.* Oval 8vo. Boston, 1807.

ION B. FORREST,

An excellent engraver in the stipple manner, was born in Aberdeenshire, Scotland,
about the year 1814. The family moving
to London, he was apprenticed to Thomas
Fry to learn the art of engraving, with
whom he remained until of age.

About the year 1837, he came to
America, and settling in Philadelphia was
engaged for "The National Portrait Gallery" and other works. He subsequently
moved to New York City, where he followed his profession, at the same time also
turning his attention to miniature painting.

He died in 1870, in Hudson County,
New Jersey.

GEORGE WASHINGTON (1772, Ætat. 40). NEARLY THREE-QUARTER LENGTH, in the costume of a Virginian Colonel. C. W. PEALE, *Pinxt.* 4to.

THOMAS JEFFERSON. HEAD AND FULL BUST. G. STUART, *Pinxt.* 8vo.

JOHN HANCOCK. FULL LENGTH SITTING at a Table, on which is an open folio vol. J. S. COPLEY, *Pinxt.* 8vo.

JOHN DICKINSON. THREE-QUARTER LENGTH STANDING, landscape back-ground. C. W. PEALE, *Pinxt.* 1770. 8vo.

COL. WILLIAM WASHINGTON. HEAD AND FULL BUST in uniform. C. W. PEALE, *Pinxt.* 8vo.

MAJOR GENERAL NATHANIEL GREENE. HEAD AND FULL BUST in uniform. J. TRUMBULL, *Pinxt.* 8vo.

THOMAS MACDONOUGH, U. S. N. HALF LENGTH STANDING in uniform. In the right distance vessels of war carrying the Am. Flag. J. W. JARVIS, *Pinxt.* 8vo.

OLIVER HAZARD PERRY, U. S. N. THREE-QUARTER LENGTH STANDING in uniform with the Am. Flag around his left arm, pointing to a vessel the hull of which is hidden in smoke. J. W. JARVIS, *Pinxt.* 8vo.

BRIG. GEN. ANTHONY WAYNE. HEAD AND BUST, wearing Mil. Hat with Cockade. J. TRUMBULL, *Pinxt.* 4to.

THOMAS GIMBREDE,

MINIATURE PAINTER and engraver, a native of France, was born in 1781. He came to America in 1802 and practiced engraving in the City of New York, working for book publishers and having several apprentices. He was appointed teacher of drawing at West Point, January 5th, 1819, which position he retained until the time of his death, which occurred December 25th, 1832.

His plates are all executed in the stipple manner, that of "The Four Presidents," from his own design, and the portrait of Commodore Perry, being very well engraved.

GEORGE WASHINGTON. HEAD AND FULL BUST. G. STUART, *Pinxt.* 8vo.

GEN. PUTNAM. HEAD AND BUST. J. TRUMBULL, *Pinxt.* 8vo.

COM'RE. OLIVER H. PERRY of the U.S. Navy. HALF LENGTH in uniform, a glass in his right hand, the arm being across the body. Upright oval with a single line of border, resting on two Dolphins. Published by MICHL. H. BOWYER, 298 Bowery, New York. Folio.

JAMES BIDDLE, Esq., of the United States Navy. HALF LENGTH in uniform. J. WOOD, *Delt.* 8vo.

LIEUT. JOHN T. SHUBRICK, late of the United States Navy. HEAD AND FULL BUST in uniform. 8vo.

HON. TIMOTHY PICKERING. HALF LENGTH. S. L. WALDO, *Pinxt.* 4to.

JOHN RANDOLPH, Esq. HEAD AND FULL BUST. JARVIS, *Pinxt.* 8vo.

DAVID RAMSAY, M.D. HEAD AND FULL BUST. J. B. WHITE, *Pinxt.* 8vo.

EDWARD S. MALBONE. HEAD AND FULL BUST. SE IPSE, *Pinxt.* 8vo.

THE FOUR PRESIDENTS. *Washington, Adams, Jefferson and Madison.* Busts in ovals grouped together in an oblong folio sheet. Over the Washington oval which is the upper one is a large star, containing thirteen smaller ones, with the words " American Star" over it. Desd., engr. and pub. by THOS. GIMBREDE, Jany. 30, 1812.

JOSEPH N. GIMBREDE,

Line and stipple engraver, son of Thomas Gimbrede, was born at West Point in the year 1820. He studied with his uncle, J. F. E. Prud'homme, but has not practiced the art for a number of years.

His plates are well and artistically engraved.

THE BATTLE AT BUNKER HILL. J. Trumbull, *Pinxt.* Ob. folio.

WASHINGTON crossing the Delaware previous to the Battle of Trenton. T. Sully, *Pinxt.* Ob. folio.

HARVESTERS NOONING. W. S. Mount, *Pinxt.* Ob. 4to.

CHRISTIAN GOBRECHT,

Was born December 23d, 1785, in Hanover, a town in York County, Pennsylvania. At an early age he exhibited considerable mechanical ability and evinced a taste for drawing and design; he was consequently apprenticed to a clockmaker living at Manheim, Lancaster County. His master, however, died a short time afterwards, when Mr. Gobrecht moved to Baltimore, for the purpose of carrying on the business, gradually passing from the ornamental work on clock faces to that of the general engraver. Commencing with the simple work of cutting headings for newspapers and punches for type founders, he became in time a writing and seal engraver, and finally a die sinker. About the year 1811, he went to Philadelphia, where his principal occupation was that of a bank note writing engraver and cutting seals and dies for book-binders. In 1836, he was appointed Die Sinker in the U. S. Mint, which office he filled until his death, which occurred July 23d, 1844.

Some of his medals were much admired, that of "The Franklin Institute,"—a head of Franklin—being extremely fine.

The portraits enumerated below are engraved in the stipple manner.

GEORGE WASHINGTON. Head and Full Bust. Stuart, *Pinxt.* 4to.

BENJAMIN FRANKLIN, LL. D., F. R. S. Half Length Sitting at a Table reading. D. Martin, *Pinxt.* 8vo.

DAVID RITTENHOUSE, LL. D., F. R. S. Half Length Sitting at a Table reading. C. W. Peale, *Pinxt.* 8vo.

DR. BENJ. S. BARTON. Head and Bust in profile. 8vo. circle.

ABRAHAM REES, D. D., F. R. S. Half Length Sitting, a manuscript in his right hand, the arm resting on a Table. Opie, R. A., *Pinxt.* Frontispiece to vol. 1, Rees' Cyclopedia, 1st Am. Ed. 4to.

CHARLES GOODMAN,

An engraver in the stipple manner, was born at Philadelphia towards the close of the last century. He studied under David

Edwin, of that city, and when nearly of age, entered into a business arrangement with a fellow-pupil, Robert Piggot, for the purpose of prosecuting portrait engraving. About the year 1819, he discontinued the art, and began the study of law. He died a member of the Philadelphia Bar in 1830.

A list of some of the works on which his name appears conjointly with his partner will be found under the head of Robert Piggot, D. D.

A. W. GRAHAM,

LINE ENGRAVER, pupil of Henry Meyer, (1783–1847), was an Englishman by birth, and came to this country about the year 1832.

His works, book plates, are well executed.

SUNSET AMONG THE ALPS. T. DOUGHTY, *Pinxt*.
Ob. 8vo.

BRADDOCK'S BATTLE FIELD. Paul Weber, *Pinxt.* Ob. 4to.

GIRARD COLLEGE for Orphans at Philada., Penna. Thomas U. Walter, archt., *Delt.* Ob. folio. Re-engraved by J. W. Steel.

GEORGE GRAHAM,

An engraver in the mezzotinto and stipple manner, but of whom no information whatever could be obtained.

MAJOR GENL. ANTHONY WAYNE. Half Length Standing in full uniform, the order of the Cincinnati on his left breast. Henry Elouis, *Pinxt.* Large folio. *Mezzotinto.*

ALEXANDER HAMILTON. Head and Full Bust in uniform. Oval in an engraved square, surrounded by Flags, &c. In a scroll at the bottom the word "Camillus." Walter Robertson, *Pinxt.* 8vo. *Stipple.*

HENRY B. HALL,

An engraver in the line and stipple manner, of much merit and ability, was born in London, March 11, 1808, and at the age of fourteen was articled as a pupil to Benjamin Smith, known by his works for "Boydell's Shakspeare Gallery." After leaving Mr. Smith he was engaged by Henry Meyer, the favorite engraver of Sir Thomas Lawrence, from whom while assisting him in his plates, he derived much instruction.

He was subsequently, for about four years, employed by H. T. Ryall, historical engraver to the Queen, engraving all the portraits in the large plates of that engraver, the "Coronation of Queen Victoria," after Sir George Hayter, being one.

Mr. Hall came to America in 1850, landing at New York in the month of December. He soon received overtures from G. P. Putnam and others for book work, and from that time has been fully employed.

His works, principally portraits, are quite numerous; we select the Washington heads and a few others as being the most interesting and also the best exponents of his art. His own portrait, executed in 1872, is a fine example of his ability as an etcher.

WASHINGTON at the age of twenty-five. HEAD AND BUST. From a miniature by J. DE MARE. Up. oval 8vo.

GEORGE WASHINGTON. HEAD AND BUST. From a pencil sketch by J. Trumbull. 4to. Private Plate.

GEORGE WASHINGTON. From the head in the Boston Athenæum. G. STUART, *Pinxt.* 4to. *Stipple.*

GEORGE WASHINGTON. HEAD AND BUST. G. STUART, *Pinxt.* Folio. Engraved in conjunction with G. E. PERINE.

GEORGE WASHINGTON. HALF LENGTH. From STUART'S portrait, painted 1796, in possession of Mr. PIERREPOINT. 4to.

GEORGE WASHINGTON. HALF LENGTH in uniform. ROBERT EDGE PINE, *Pinxt.* 1785. 4to. *Stipple.*

GEORGE WASHINGTON. HEAD AND BUST. A. WERTMULLER, *Pinxt.* 1795. 4to. *Stipple.*

GEORGE WASHINGTON. Profile Head. From a miniature painted from life by JAMES SHARPLESS in 1796. 8vo. Private Plate.

GEORGE WASHINGTON. Head and Bust. J. Peale, *Pinxt.* 1788. 8vo. Private Plate.

GEORGE WASHINGTON. Head and Bust. Rembrandt Peale, *Pinxt.* 4to.

GEORGE WASHINGTON. Profile from the Bust by G. Ceracchi. 8vo.

GEORGE WASHINGTON. Profile from the Bust by Houdon. 8vo.

BENEDICT ARNOLD. Profile Head. 4to. Private Plate.

JAMES DUANE. Head and Bust. Etched. 8vo. Private Plate.

THOMAS SULLY. Head and Bust. Drawn and etched by H. B. Hall, 1869. 8vo. Private Plate.

HENRY B. HALL. Head and Full Bust, head supported by right hand. *Se ipse delt.* Etched 1872.

GEORGE R. HALL,

An engraver in the line and stipple manner, was born in London in the year 1818, and commenced his studies under his brother, H. B. Hall, at the age of fourteen. On leaving him he worked for other engravers for a year or two, and then went to Leipsic, Germany, to fill an engagement for three years with A. H. Payne, engraver and publisher of that city.

At the end of that time he returned to London, and a few years afterwards came to America, arriving at New York in 1854, having previously entered into an agreement with the Bank Note engraving firm of Rawdon, Wright, Hatch & Co., of that city.

Since leaving them he has been engaged by the different publishing houses of New York.

Among his book plates those for Irving's Life of Washington, after designs by F. O. C. Darley, may be cited as good examples of his abilities as a draughtsman and engraver.

WASHINGTON'S ADIEU TO HIS GENERALS.
F. O. C. DARLEY, *Delt.*   Imp. folio.

WASHINGTON'S FIRST INTERVIEW WITH HIS WIFE.   J. W. EHNINGER, *Pinxt.*   Imp. folio.

THE NATIVITY. CHRISTMAS MORNING. ALONZO CHAPPEL, *Pinxt.* Imp. folio.

FREDERICK HALPIN,

LINE and Stipple engraver, was born in the city of Worcester, England, in 1805, and acquired the elements of the art under his father, who followed the business of an engraver in the Staffordshire Potteries.

After his father's decease, which took place in London when Mr. Halpin was about twenty-two years of age, he turned his attention to pictorial engraving, which he has since followed.

He came to America in 1842, and settled in New York City, where he now resides. Mr. Halpin is a fine draughtsman and an admirable engraver. His portrait of John F. Kensett will compare, for taste and excellence of execution, with the best productions of the day.

ABRAHAM LINCOLN. HEAD AND BUST.   From Life by F. B. CARPENTER, 1864.   Folio.

ASHER B. DURAND. HEAD AND FULL BUST.   C. L. ELLIOTT, *Pinxt.*   4to.

JOHN F. KENSETT. HEAD AND FULL BUST.   GEO. A. BAKER, N. A., *Pinxt.*   4to.   Pub. N. Y. 1869.

REV. SAMUEL OSGOOD. HEAD AND FULL BUST. THOMAS LE CLEAR, *Pinxt.*   4to.

THE NURSE. EASTMAN JOHNSON, *Delt.*   Roy. folio.

GEORGE W. HATCH,

LINE ENGRAVER, was born in the western part of the State of New York, and studied under A. B. Durand.   He was a good designer and engraver, his Bank Note vignettes being held in much esteem.

He was one of the firm of Rawdon, Wright, Hatch & Co., Bank Note engravers of New York, and is deceased.

ROBERT HINSHELWOOD,

LANDSCAPE ENGRAVER, was born at Edinburgh in 1812.   When about eleven years of age, he was placed with James and John Johnstone, of that city, to learn the art and craft of engraving, during his stay with them attending as a pupil at the Royal Academy, and studying drawing under Sir William Allan.

His instruction in engraving was very slight, the source for information being extremely limited. He, however, remained with them for seven years, and about the year 1832 came to America, settled in New York City, and commenced working for the Harper Bros. and other publishers.

Mr. Hinshelwood's plates are engraved with much taste and ability, and in the spirit of a true artist, he seeks to translate the picture rather than to exhibit his own talent and manipulation. Very few engravers of the country have produced anything more artistic than several of his late productions, such as "Moonrise at

6

Sunset," after De Haas, and "The Pet Lamb," after Eastman Johnson.

EVENING. W. L. SONNTAG, *Pinxt.* Ob. 4to.

THE RIVER-SIDE PATH (A Glimpse of the Catskills). J. W. CASILEAR, *Pinxt.* 4to.

THE LAST GLEAM. W. HART, *Pinxt.* Ob. 4to.

WINTER'S CHARMS. J. McENTEE, *Pinxt.* 4to.

CROSSING THE DESERT. M. DUVIEUX, *Pinxt.* Ob. 4to.

SUMMER WOODS. JAS. M. HART, *Pinxt.* 4to.

HOMEWARD BOUND. JAS. M. HART, *Pinxt.* 4to.

MOONRISE AT SUNSET. M. F. H. DeHAAS, *Pinxt.* Ob. 4to.

MOONLIGHT AT SEA. M. F. H. DeHAAS, *Pinxt.* 4to.

TRENTON FALLS, N. Y. J. F. KENSETT, *Pinxt.* Folio.

SPRING. J. F. KENSETT, *Pinxt.*

CHOCORUA PEAK (White Mountains). J. W. CASILEAR, *Pinxt.* Folio.

THE PET LAMB. EASTMAN JOHNSON, *Pinxt.* Ob. Roy. folio.

WILLIAM HOOGLAND,

MENTIONED in the Biography of Joseph Andrews as being the first instructor of that engraver, and as practicing the art in the city of Boston in the year 1825.

WM. E. CHANNING. CHESTER HARDING, *Pinxt.* Folio.

JOHN RYLAND, D. D. FULL BUST. N. BRANWHITE, *Pinxt.* 8vo. *Stipple.*

ALEXANDER HAMILTON. HALF LENGTH. AMES, *Pinxt.* 8vo. *Stipple.*

H. HOUSTON,

AN engraver in the stipple manner, but of whom no information could be obtained.

The three prints enumerated below, published in Philadelphia in the early part of the century, are well engraved.

GENERAL WASHINGTON, Pres. of the U. S. of

Am. HEAD AND BUST. J. J. BARRALET, *Delt.* Oval in a rectangle. Large folio.

GEORGE WASHINGTON, Esq. HEAD AND BUST in uniform. Philada. Pub. by Thos. CONDIE, Book Seller. Oval 8vo.

HIS EXCELLENCY, JOHN ADAMS, President of the United States of America. THREE-QUARTER LENGTH SITTING, both hands resting upon an up. vol., which is on his knees. H. HOUSTON SE IPSE, *Delt.* Small folio. Pub. by D. KENNEDY, 228 Market St. Philada.

WILLIAM HUMPHREYS.

THIS admirable line engraver was a native of Ireland, born at Dublin in 1794, but came to America quite early in life, and learned the art of engraving from George Murray, of Philadelphia.

While in this country he produced numerous small plates for annuals and illustrated books, such as editions of Bryant and Longfellow, his principal employment however being on vignettes for bank notes, in which direction he was particularly successful.

His best and largest works were executed in England, where he went in 1822, only returning to this country about 1843, for a visit of two years' duration.

His plates are executed in the very best manner and with much taste and faithfulness of translation, that of "Sancho and the Duchess," after C. R. Leslie, being extremely happy in conveying the exquisite humor and artistic excellence of the original.

William Humphreys died January 21st, 1865, at Villa Novella, Genoa, where he had gone in the hope of restoring his health.

WASHINGTON. HALF LENGTH. From a picture by GILBERT STUART, in the possession of T. B. BARCLAY, Esq., of Liverpool. 8vo.

THE EARLY DAYS OF WASHINGTON. II. INMAN, *Pinxt.* Ob. 8vo.

PRECIOSA BEFORE THE ARCHBISHOP. D. Huntington, *Pinxt.* 8vo.

EXCELSIOR. D. Huntington, *Pinxt.* 8vo.

THE NECKLACE. C. R. Leslie, *Pinxt.* 8vo.

MARC BEAN CREEK, GEORGIA. Joshua Shaw, *Pinxt.* 4to.

SPANISH PEASANT BOY. Murillo, *Pinxt.* London, 1833. 4to.

SANCHO AND THE DUCHESS. C. R. Leslie, *Pinxt.* London, 1838. Ob. Roy. folio.

LA MADDALENA. Correggio, *Pinxt.* Copy of Longhi's print. London, 1839. Ob. folio.

THE COQUETTE. Sir Joshua Reynolds, *Pinxt.* London, 1849. Folio.

SAMUEL V. HUNT,

Landscape engraver, was born in Norwich, England, February 14th, 1803.

Mr. Hunt never received any regular instruction in the art, and previously to his arrival in this country (1834), had seen but one steel plate, having been chiefly occupied in preserving animals and birds, occasionally painting and etching.

His first plates were executed for the "Book of the Picturesque," published by G. P. Putnam, from pictures by Church, Huntington, Weir and others. He has also engraved for "Picturesque America," published by Appleton and Co., and is at present engaged upon a companion work by the same publishers, entitled "Picturesque Europe."

His plates are beautifully and delicately engraved and in fine artistic feeling.

WA WA YANDA. D. Huntington, *Pinxt.* 4to.

A MORNING IN THE TROPICS. F. E. Church, *Pinxt.* 4to.

NOON ON THE SEA SHORE. J. F. Kensett, *Pinxt.* 4to.

THE RIVER ROAD. A. F. Bellows, *Pinxt.* 4to.

SILVER LAKE. A. Bierstadt, *Pinxt.* Roy. folio.

THE NURSE. Eastman Johnson, *Delt.* Roy. folio. Engraved in conjunction with F. Halpin.

NATHANIEL HURD,

PROBABLY the first practitioner of the art of engraving in the United States, was born in Boston the thirteenth day of February, 1730, where he died December 17th, 1777.

His regular vocation was seal cutting and die engraving, in which he is said to have excelled.

PORTRAIT OF THE REV. DR. SEWALL, Minister of the Old South Church, Boston. From a miniature. Engraved in 1764.

A CARICATURE PRINT representing Doctor Seth Hudson and a certain Mr. Howe, convicted of forging and uttering "province notes," the former in the pillory and the latter at the whipping post. Engraved in 1762. "Sold by N. Hurd, near the Exchange, at the Heart and Crown, in Cornhill, Boston."

ALFRED JONES.

THIS admirable line engraver was born

in Liverpool, England, April 7, 1819, but came to this country quite early in life.

An inherent love for drawing inducing some amateur attempts at engraving, led him to adopt the profession, and at the age of fifteen (1834), he entered the Bank Note Establishment of Rawdon, Wright, Hatch and Edson, first at Albany and subsequently at New York. While with them he attended the Antique School of the National Academy of Design, and in 1839, received the first prize for a drawing from Thorwaldsen's Mercury.

His first plate, engraved on his own account and bearing his name, was executed about the year 1841 for Godey's Magazine, that and Graham's being the popular periodicals of the day. For the latter he also produced some plates, one named "The Proposal" leading to an acquaintance with the artist, A. B. Durand, at that time the adviser in matters of engraving of the American Art Union, at whose instance he was engaged to engrave the plate of "Farmers' Nooning," after W. S. Mount, for the subscribers of the year 1843, to be followed by others hereafter mentioned.

During the years 1846–47, he visited Europe, meeting in London with some of the best English engravers, and while in Paris studying at the life schools of that city. Upon his return he was engaged on some large plates for the Western Art Union, "Poor Relations," after J. H. Beard, and one after Mrs. Lillie M. Spencer, done in the mixed manner. Since 1850, he has been almost exclusively engaged on bank note vignettes, producing some of the choicest examples of the art.

Mr. Jones was elected associate member of the National Academy of Design in

1841, and an academician in 1851, and is now its recording secretary. He paints occasionally in oil and water colors, and is a member of the Artist Fund and Water Color Societies of New York.

Alfred Jones is one of the best line engravers now working in America. His plates, executed in an artistic manner, show fine drawing and burin work, accuracy of detail and good general effect. "The Image Breaker," after E. Leutze, is an admirable production.

ADONIRAM JUDSON, Missionary to Burmah. HALF LENGTH SITTING, right hand lying on a folio vol. entitled "Holy Bible in Burmese." CHESTER HARDING, *Pinxt.* Pub. for Am. Baptist Miss. Union, 1846. 4to.

WILLIAM CULLEN BRYANT. HEAD AND FULL BUST. Up. oval in a rectangle. A. B. DURAND, *Pinxt.* Engraved in conjunction with S. A. SCHOFF. Pub. by "The Century," 1858. Folio.

THE CAPTURE OF MAJOR ANDRE. A. B. DURAND, *Pinxt,* The landscape engraved by SMILLIE & HINSHELWOOD. Am. Art Union Print, 1845. Ob. large folio.

SPARKING. J. W. Edmonds, *Pinxt.* Am. Art Union Print, 1845. Ob. large folio.

THE IMAGE BREAKER. E. Leutze, *Pinxt.* Am. Art Union Print, 1850. 4to.

THE NEW SCHOLAR. J. W. Edmonds, *Pinxt.* Am. Art Union Print, 1850. Ob. 4to.

MEXICAN NEWS. R. C. Woodville, *Pinxt.* Am. Art Union Print, 1851. Roy. folio. *Mixed style.*

PATRICK HENRY, delivering his celebrated speech in the House of Burgesses, Virginia, 1765. P. F. Rothermel, *Pinxt.* Am. Art Union of Philad'a, 1852. Imp. folio.

FRANCIS KEARNY,

A line engraver of some merit, was born at Perth Amboy, New Jersey, about the year 1780. At the age of eighteen, having shown a predilection for drawing and engraving, he was placed with Peter R. Maverick, of New York, an engraver of repute at that time and with whom he remained for three years.

On arriving at age he commenced business, as an engraver, for himself, his first plate, of any account, being executed for an encyclopedia published by John Law, of New York. In the year 1810, he moved to Philadelphia, where he found constant employment, that city at the time being far beyond New York in book publishing, engraving and the like.

In 1820, he entered into partnership with Benjamin Tanner and others, for the term of three years, the object being bank note engraving. The title of the firm was Tanner, Vallance, Kearny and Co. At the expiration of this partnership, he worked for Souvenirs and other publications, principally religious subjects. The time of his decease could not be ascertained.

CHIEF JUSTICE MARSHALL, HALF LENGTH in judicial robes, sitting at a table writing. 8vo. *Stipple.*

THE LAST SUPPER. LEONARD DA VINCI, *Pinxt.* Pub. in 1833. Copy of Raphael Morghen's Print. Ob. roy. folio.

VIEW NEAR TICONDEROGA. Thos. Cole, *Pinxt.* 8vo.

THOMAS KELLY,

An excellent line engraver, was an Irishman by birth, but acquired his art in the city of Boston. He practiced in Philadelphia about 1830, being then thirty-five years of age. A few years subsequently, he went to New York, where he died.

WASHINGTON. Full Length in uniform. From G. Stuart's picture in Faneuil Hall, Boston. Pub. 1836. Roy. folio.

THOMAS JEFFERSON. Half Length Sitting. Otis, *Pinxt.* 8vo. *Stipple.*

FISHER AMES. Half Length Sitting. G. Stuart, *Pinxt.* 8vo.

RUFUS KING. Half Length Sitting. G. Stuart, *Pinxt.* 8vo.

LOUIS McLANE. Head and Full Bust. G. S. Newton, *Pinxt.* 8vo.

PHILIP SCHUYLER, Major General U. S. A. Head and Full Bust in uniform. J. Trumbull, *Pinxt.* 8vo.

EDWARD PREBLE, U. S. N. HALF LENGTH in uniform. 8vo.

N, CHAPMAN, M. D. THREE-QUARTER LENGTH STANDING at a Table, wearing an overcoat. Architectural background. J. NEAGLE, *Pinxt.* Pub. 1831. Folio.

THE VILLAGE BLACKSMITH AT HIS FORGE. Portrait of Pat. Lyon the celebrated Philadelphia Blacksmith. JOHN NEAGLE, *Pinxt.* 8vo.

GEORGE S. LANG,

OF Scotch descent, was born in Chester County, Pennsylvania, in 1799. In his fourteenth year he was apprenticed to George Murray, of Philadelphia, with whom he remained until of age, during which time, with the exception of working on some plates for Rees' Cyclopedia, he was principally employed on bank-note work.

He abandoned engraving for trade shortly after becoming twenty-one, the only large plate executed by him, with the exception of an unfinished one of "The First Landing of Columbus in the New World," after a design by J. J. Barralet, is the one mentioned below.

He has retired from the business and is living in Delaware County, Pennsylvania.

WASHINGTON passing the Delaware the evening previous to the Battle of Trenton, Dec. 25, 1776. T. Sully, *Pinxt.* Ob. folio. *Line.* The figures etched by W. Humphreys.

ALEXANDER LAWSON.

This admirable line engraver and most excellent man was born December 19th, 1772, at Ravenstruthers, a village in Lanarkshire, Scotland. His passion for art evinced itself at an early period of life. Being left an orphan at fifteen, he went to reside with an elder brother, at Liverpool, who much desired that he should devote himself to mercantile pursuits and opposed his decided inclination to engraving, which he persevered in attempting in the hours not required by the business demands of his brother's establishment.

Loving art better than trade and taking views of political questions, quite different from those of his brother, he determined to go to America, and arrived at Baltimore in May, 1792, where he remained but a few days before going to Philadelphia, in which city he finally settled.

His first works of any consequence were four plates for Thompson's Seasons, executed for Thos. Dobson, bookseller, which attracted much notice. Some time in the year 1798, Mr. Lawson formed a friendship with Alexander Wilson, for whose work on ornithology, and its continuation by Charles Lucien Bonaparte, he engraved all the best plates. The late John Neagle, the eminent portrait painter, was accustomed to term him "the best engraver of birds in America."

He also engraved some plates for a proposed work on quadrupeds, by the late George Ord, a work on conchology, by Prof. Haldeman, and another on the same subject, by Dr. Amos Binney, the drawings for the two latter works being made by Mr. Lawson's second daughter.

Extremely industrious and of immense application, his works are very numerous, including plates for annuals, maps, charts, illustrations of works on chemistry, botany, mineralogy, etc., all executed in the best manner.

He pursued his art until within ten days of his death, which happened at Philadelphia on the twenty-second day of August, 1846.

GEORGE WASHINGTON. Head and Bust in an oval. G. Stuart, *Pinxt.* 8vo. *Stipple and line.*

ROBERT BURNS. HEAD AND BUST in an oval. A.
NASMYTH, *Pinxt.* 8vo.

MRS. SUSANNAH POULSON. HEAD AND FULL
BUST. JAS. PEALE, *Pinxt.* Engd. in 1831. 8vo.

**PERRY'S VICTORY ON LAKE ERIE, Sept. 10,
1813**. T. BIRCH, *Pinxt.* Ob. Roy. folio.

MACPHERSON'S BLUES TAKING LEAVE.
A crack corps of Philada. organized 1794, to quell the
resistance to the Revenue Laws in Penna., known as
the "Whiskey Insurrection." BARRALET, *Delt.* Small
folio. *Stipple.*

ELECTION DAY IN PHILADELPHIA. A Scene
in front of the State House. J. L. KRIMMEL, *Pinxt.*
Ob. imp. folio. Left unfinished, three impressions only
were taken after the decease of the engraver.

MY UNCLE TOBY AND THE WIDOW. C. R.
LESLIE, *Pinxt.* 8vo.

THE PAINTER'S STUDY. W. S. MOUNT, *Pinxt.*
8vo.

THE RAFFLE. W. S. MOUNT, *Pinxt.* 8vo.

THE SNARE. J. G. CHAPMAN, *Pinxt.* 8vo.

THE HAPPY FAMILY. (Return from Market).
J. L. KRIMMEL, *Pinxt.* 8vo.

PAST, PRESENT AND FUTURE. Three female
figures of much beauty, THREE-QUARTER LENGTHS. 8vo.

NEOTOMA FLORIDANA. The Florida Rat.
Engraved for the journal of the Acad. of Natural
Sciences, Philada. C. A. LESUER, *Delt.* Small 4to.

THE GREAT AMERICAN ELK. 4to.

OSCAR A. LAWSON,

LINE ENGRAVER, son and pupil of Alexander Lawson, was born at Philadelphia August 7th, 1813.

In 1841, he entered the office of the U. S. Coast Survey, at Washington City, where he remained until 1851, when he returned to his native place in ill-health.

His engravings, mostly book plates, are executed with taste and ability.

He died September 6th, 1854.

AUDREY AND TOUCHSTONE. C. R. LESLIE, *Pinxt.* Ob. 8vo.

THE INDIGENT FAMILY. PRUD'HON, *Pinxt.* 8vo.

THE DEATH SCENE. PRUDHON, *Pinxt.* 8vo.

TEACHING THE SCRIPTURE. J. PORTER, *Delt.* 8vo.

THE DEATH OF ADDISON. S. W. REYNOLDS, *Pinxt.* 8vo.

THE OLD SOLDIER. R. FARRIER, *Pinxt.* 8vo.

JOHN ANDERSON, MY JO. W. KIDD, *Pinxt.* 8vo.

HAVERFORD SCHOOL HOUSE, DEL. COY. PA. Front view. Se ipse, *Delt.* 4to.

WILLIAM S. LENEY,

An excellent draughtsman and engraver in the stipple manner, was born in London and acquired the art under P. W. Tomkins. He executed several large plates before coming to this country, including an excellent one of "The Descent from the Cross," after Rubens. Settling in New York at the beginning of the century, he entered into partnership with William Rollinson, for bank-note engraving, was successful and retired with a competency.

He subsequently purchased a farm on the river St. Lawrence, a little below Montreal, where he died.

JOHN ADAMS. Head and Full Bust. J. S. Copley, *Pinxt.* 8vo.

PATRICK HENRY. HEAD AND FULL BUST. T. SULLY, *Pinxt.* Pub. 1817. 8vo.

JAMES LAWRENCE, Esq., late Capt. in the U. S. Navy. Obit. in Frigate Chesapeake, June 5, 1813. Ætat. 32. HEAD AND FULL BUST in Uniform. In the lower Margin the words, "Don't give up the Ship." G. STUART, *Pinxt.* 8vo.

DEWITT CLINTON. HALF LENGTH SITTING. J. TRUMBULL, *Pinxt.* 8vo.

JOHN JAY, Esq. THREE-QUARTER LENGTH. G. STUART, *Pinxt.* 8vo.

HON. THEOPHILUS PARSONS. HEAD AND FULL BUST. G. STUART, *Pinxt.* 8vo. *line.*

ROBERT FULTON, Esq. HEAD AND FULL BUST. B. WEST, *Pinxt.* 8vo.

RUFUS KING, Esq. HEAD AND FULL BUST. WOOD, *Pinxt.* 8vo.

JAMES B. LONGACRE,

A DESCENDANT from the early Swedish settlers upon the banks of the Delaware, the family name having been originally Longker, was born in Delaware County, Pennsylvania, August 11th, 1794, and died at Philadelphia January 1st, 1869.

He served his apprenticeship as an engraver with George Murray, of that city, and from 1819 to 1831 was employed on illustrations for some of the best works then issuing from the American Press.

In conjunction with James Herring, portrait painter, of New York, he began the publication of the widely known "National Portrait Gallery of Distinguished Americans," four volumes, large 8vo, 1834–1839, which he afterwards continued alone. Some of the portraits in the work were from his own drawings from the life, the very best talent of the time being enlisted to write the lives, numbering one hundred and forty-four, a few being autobiographies. The work contains one hundred and forty-seven portraits, twenty-four of which were engraved by himself.

The enterprise and patriotism which enabled him to carry on to completion, under unusual difficulties, a work the first of its character of any importance undertaken in this country, entitle him to be honorably mentioned by all interested in perpetuating the features of the prominent men of our early history.

He worked in line and the stipple manner, and was an excellent engraver. Many of his portraits possess considerable merit; that of Charles Carroll, of Carrollton, after Chester Harding, is a fine specimen of the art, the head being particularly well engraved.

During the last twenty-five years of his life (1844–1869), he was engraver to the United States Mint. The new coins, struck during that period—the double eagle, the three dollar piece, the gold dollar, etc.,—were made by him from his own designs.

GEORGE WASHINGTON. HEAD AND FULL BUST. G. STUART, *Pinxt.* 8vo.

MARTHA WASHINGTON. HEAD AND BUST. From a miniature by Robertson. 8vo.

JOHN ADAMS. HEAD AND FULL BUST. G. STUART, *Pinxt.* 8vo.

JOHN HANCOCK. HEAD AND FULL BUST. J. S. COPLEY, *Pinxt.* 8vo.

THOMAS JEFFERSON. HEAD AND FULL BUST. G. STUART, *Pinxt.* 8vo.

BENJAMIN FRANKLIN. HALF LENGTH SITTING at a Table reading. MARTIN, *Pinxt.* 8vo.

CHARLES CARROLL OF CARROLLTON. HALF LENGTH SITTING, a book in his right hand. CHESTER HARDING, *Pinxt.* Folio. *Line.*

DAVID RITTENHOUSE. HALF LENGTH SITTING at a Table on which is a chart to which he is pointing. C. W. PEALE, *Pinxt.* 8vo.

FRANCIS HOPKINSON. HALF LENGTH SITTING at a Table writing. PINE, *Pinxt.* 8vo.

JOHN QUINCY ADAMS. HEAD AND FULL BUST. G. STUART, *Pinxt.* 4to.

MAJOR GENERAL ALEXANDER MACOMB. HEAD AND FULL BUST, in uniform, the arms folded. T. SULLY, *Pinxt.* 8vo.

JOHN BARRY, U. S. N. HEAD AND FULL BUST in uniform. G. STUART, *Pinxt.* 8vo. *Line.*

JOHN PAUL JONES. HEAD AND FULL BUST in uniform and chapeau. C. W. PEALE, *Pinxt.* 8vo.

DANIEL BOONE. HALF LENGTH attired in a hunting-shirt trimmed with fur, a buck-horn handled hunting-knife stuck in his belt. CHESTER HARDING, *Pinxt.* 8vo.

THOMAS MCKEAN, GOV. OF PENNA. HEAD AND FULL BUST, on the left breast the order of the Cincinnati. G. STUART, *Pinxt.* 8vo.

BUSHROD WASHINGTON, Ass. Justice S. C. U. S. HEAD AND FULL BUST in judicial gown. CHESTER HARDING, *Pinxt.* Folio.

MAJ. GEN. ANDREW JACKSON. HALF LENGTH STANDING in uniform and military over-coat. His left arm and hand rest on a horse in the rear, the head and neck of which are only visible, in his right hand a sword. THOS. SULLY, *Pinxt.* Pub. Nov. 2, 1820. Folio.

MAJ. GENL. ANDREW JACKSON. HALF LENGTH wearing a cloak. The border resembles a picture frame. J. WOOD, *Pinxt.* 4to.

JOHN C. CALHOUN. HEAD AND FULL BUST. C. B. KING, *Pinxt.* 8vo.

WILLIAM T. BARRY. HEAD AND FULL BUST. J. B. LONGACRE, *Delt.* Pub. 1833. Folio.

ROBERT Y. HAYNE. HEAD AND FULL BUST. J. B. LONGACRE, *Delt.* Pub. 1840. Folio.

NICHOLAS BIDDLE. HALF LENGTH SITTING, right arm resting upon a table. REMBRANDT PEALE, *Pinxt.* Engraved in conjunction with Thos. B. Welch. 8vo.

REV. ROBERT R. ROBERTS, Bishop M. E. Church. HALF LENGTH. J. NEAGLE, *Pinxt.* 8vo.

REV. H. B. BASCOM, Bishop M. E. Church. HALF LENGTH. J. NEAGLE, *Pinxt.* 1826. Engraved, 1829. 4to.

MOST REV. AMBROSE MARESCHAL, Third Archbishop of Baltimore. HALF LENGTH in robes. P. TILYARD, *Pinxt.* Folio.

REV. SAMUEL B. WYLIE, D. D. HEAD AND FULL BUST, hands and arms only indicated. J. NEAGLE, *Pinxt.* 4to.

PHILIP SYNG PHYSICK, M. D. HEAD AND BUST. From a sketch by T. SULLY. Folio.

C. W. PEALE. HALF LENGTH SITTING, Palette and Brushes in his left hand. REMBRANDT PEALE, *Pinxt.* 8vo.

SIR WALTER SCOTT. HALF LENGTH SITTING, a walking stick in his right hand, and a Scotch cap or bonnet in the left. C. R. LESLIE, *Pinxt.* 8vo. *Line.*

JAMES PELLER MALCOM,

DRAUGHTSMAN and line engraver, was born at Philadelphia in August, 1767. Upon arriving at age, he visited England and studied painting for three years at the

Royal Academy. Finding no employment in the art, he returned to Philadelphia, and took up the graver without any previous instruction. After a short residence in his native city, he again went to England, and was engaged on works chiefly of a topographical nature.

He executed quite a number of plates for the Gentleman's Magazine, and for some publications of his own, such as "Excursions through Kent," and "Anecdotes of the Manners and Customs of London during the 18th Century," published in 1808.

He died in London April 5th, 1815.

CHRIST CHURCH, Philad'a. (Interior view). Designed and engraved by J. P. M. 1787. 4to.

CHRIST CHURCH, Philad'a. (Exterior view). Des. & Eng. by J. P. M. 8vo.

BUSH HILL, the seat of Wm. Hamilton, Esq., near Philad'a. Des. & Eng. by J. P. M. Pub. in the Universal Magazine, London, 1787.

WILLIAM E. MARSHALL.

THIS admirable line engraver was born in the City of New York on the thirtieth day of June, 1836.

His first works to attract attention were a series of vignettes executed for Danforth, Wright and Co., bank note engravers, which induced overtures from the " National Bank Note Co.," then about being organized, and for which he produced for the first three years of its existence all its vignettes and portraits.

In the winter of 1860, he went to Boston to engrave the head of Washington, from Stuart's painting in the Athenæum, and after its completion, went abroad to study painting. While busily engaged with the brush at Paris, in 1865, he heard of the assassination of President

Lincoln, and immediately returned to his native country, for the purpose of engraving his portrait, the picture to be painted by himself.

Marshall's head, of J. Fennimore Cooper, executed with much freedom and ability, is a fine example of engraved portraiture, and his Washington stands deservedly high in the estimation of good judges.

HEAD OF CHRIST. After Leonardo Da Vinci. 8vo. Engraved for Henry Ward Beecher's life of Christ.

GEORGE WASHINGTON. From the Head by G. Stuart in the Boston Athenæum. Folio. Pub. 1862.

ABRAHAM LINCOLN. Head and Bust. Up. Oval with border in an engraved rectangle. W. E. Marshall, *Pinxt.* Roy. folio. Pub. 1866.

GEN. U. S. GRANT. Head and Bust. Up. oval with border in an engraved rectangle. W. E. Marshall, *Pinxt.* Roy. folio. Pub. 1868.

J. FENNIMORE COOPER. Head and Bust. C. L. Elliott, *Pinxt.* 4to.

HENRY WARD BEECHER. Head and Bust. Up. Oval with border in an engraved rectangle. W. E. Marshall, *Pinxt.* Roy. folio.

PETER R. MAVERICK,

An American by birth, born on the 11th day of April, 1755, was originally a silversmith. He etched and engraved for many years in New York, and by being the teacher of his son Peter and of Francis Kearny, aided materially in the progress of American engraving.

The plates executed by him, for Brown's Family Bible, published by Hodge, Allen and Campbell, in New York, are said to be the best specimens of his art. (Dunlap, Hist. of the Arts of Design in the U. S.)

PETER MAVERICK,

Son of Peter R. Maverick, was born in the City of New York, October 22d, 1780, and died there June 7th, 1831. He was a prominent engraver of his time, having many pupils, among whom was included Asher B. Durand.

He acquired the art under his father, and worked principally for book publishers and bank note companies.

The portraits referred to below are well engraved in line.

HENRY CLAY. HALF LENGTH SITTING at a Table holding in his right hand a strip of paper on which is inscribed his Resolution (offered in Congress, Feb'y 10, 1821) of sympathy and interest for the success of the Spanish Provinces of South America in their struggle for independence. CHAS. KING, *Pinxt.* Pub. at Washington City, 1822. Folio.

MAJ. GEN. ANDREW JACKSON. HEAD AND BUST. S. L. WALDO, *Pinxt.* 4to.

THE RIGHT REV. RICHARD CHANNING MOORE, D. D. Bishop of the P. E. Church, Va. HALF LENGTH SITTING in robes holding in his left hand an open volume from which by the action of the extended right hand he is reading aloud. WM. DUNLAP, *Pinxt.* Roy. folio. Pub. New York, 1823.

CADWALLADER D. COLDEN, Esq., Mayor of the City of New York. HEAD AND FULL BUST. WALDO & JEWETT, *Pinxt.* Engraved by P. Maverick, and Durand & Co. 4to.

JOHN McGOFFIN,

ENGRAVER in the line and mixed manner, was born in Philadelphia in 1813, and was a pupil of James W. Steel, of that city, with whom he remained until twenty-one years of age. He practiced miniature painting for eleven or twelve years after coming of age, but after that time, returned to engraving, which he has since regularly prosecuted.

Mr. McGoffin has been principally employed by book publishers. His plates are well executed and in good keeping.

He has lately engraved, from a design by H. J. Schwartzman, a beautiful vignette plate of the Art Gallery, "Memorial Hall," of "The United States Centennial International Exhibition."

8

PETER MORAN,

ANIMAL PAINTER, was born on the Fourth day of March, 1842, in Lancashire, England, and was brought to this country when about two years of age, the family settling in Philadelphia.

In the studio of his brothers, Edward and Thomas Moran, he imbibed a taste for art, commencing as a marine painter, which branch, however, after two years' practice, being then nineteen years of age, was discontinued for animal life, which he has since pursued. A close student of nature, his pictures are well and truthfully composed, and executed in fine tone and feeling.

In the early part of the present year (1875) Mr. Moran took up the etching needle with much enthusiasm, and has already produced some excellent examples of this fascinating branch of art. He is the first painter to practice in this country to any extent this charming specialty.

The "Chariot Race in the Circus Maximus," in conjunction with S. J. Ferris, executed in a free, artistic manner, is the most important etching yet produced in America.

TRAVELLERS ATTACKED BY WOLVES. R. ANSDELL, *Pinxt.* Ob. folio.

OXEN PLOUGHING. ROSA BONHEUR, *Pinxt.* Ob. 4to.

CHARIOT RACE in the Circus Maximus, Rome, in the presence of the Emperor Domitian. A. WAGNER, *Pinxt.* Etched in conjunction with S. J. Ferris. Ob. Roy. folio.

THE COMING STORM. Orig. design. Ob. folio.

THE SHADY LANE. Orig. design. 4to.

A SET OF TWELVE. Landscape and Animal Subjects. Orig. designs. 4to.

GEORGE MURRAY,

THE senior member of the well-known

Bank-note engraving firm of Murray, Draper, Fairman & Co., was a native of Scotland, but went to London when quite young, and was taught engraving by that admirable artist, Anker Smith.

Becoming entangled in the politics of the day, he found it prudent to leave England and come to America, landing in the Southern States, where he married and commenced as a trader. Having failed in his efforts in this direction, he removed his family to Philadelphia about the year 1800, and resuming his profession, found employment from the Book Publishers of the day. He was particularly skilled in animals; his plate of a Lion, Lioness and young, engraved for Rees' Cyclopedia, after a design by S. Edwards, is a fine example of the art.

In 1811 the Bank-note engraving firm above mentioned was formed, which was extremely successful, Murray being the financier and apparent leader of the business. He was, however, reckless and improvident in speculations and manner of living, and died poor somewhere about the year 1823.

The two prints mentioned below, executed in line, bear the name of Murray, Draper, Fairman & Co., as Engravers.

THE BATTLE ON LAKE ERIE, Fought, Sept., **10, 1813**. FIRST VIEW. SULLY AND KEARNY, *Delt.* Ob. Roy. folio.

THE BATTLE ON LAKE ERIE, Fought Sept. **10, 1813**. SECOND VIEW. SULLY AND KEARNY, *Delt.* Ob. Roy. folio.

JOHN B. NEAGLE,

LINE ENGRAVER, son of John Neagle, an English engraver, came to America when quite young, and settled in Philadelphia, where he died in 1866, being about sixty-five years of age.

His plates, principally for Annuals, are well executed. During the latter part of his life he was mostly engaged on Bank note work.

THOMAS JEFFERSON. Half length, sitting, hands, folded in front. OTIS, *Pinxt.* 8vo.

HENRY LAURENS. HEAD AND FULL BUST. C. W. PEALE, *Pinxt.* 8vo.

NATHANIEL CHAPMAN, M. D. HALF LENGTH STANDING, as if speaking. THOS. SULLY, *Pinxt.* 8vo.

THE DUTCH MAIDEN. G. S. NEWTON, *Pinxt.* 8vo.

THE INDIAN TOILET. J. G. CHAPMAN, *Pinxt.* 8vo.

THE WRECKED MARINER. T. BIRCH, *Delt.* 8vo.

THE WOLF AND THE LAMB. W. MULREADY, *Pinxt.* A copy of J. H. Robinson's print. 8vo.

PHILADELPHIA. (View of). J. R. SMITH, *Delt.* Ob. 4to.

BALTIMORE. (View of). J. R. SMITH, *Delt.* Ob. 4to.

JOHN W. PARADISE,

LINE ENGRAVER, son of John Paradise, Portrait Painter, (1783–1833,) was a pupil of A. B. Durand, with whom he entered about

the year 1825. He engraved some plates
for "The National Portrait Gallery," and
was afterwards principally occupied on
small Portraits and Vignettes for Bank
note Establishments in the city of New
York. Is deceased.

MORGAN LEWIS. THREE-QUARTER LENGTH SITTING.
  JAS HERRING, *Pinxt.* Engraved in conjunction with
  A. B. Durand. 8vo.

JOHN QUINCY ADAMS. HALF LENGTH. A. B.
  DURAND, *Pinxt.* 8vo.

ELIAS DEXTER. HALF LENGTH. J. T. PEELE, *Pinxt.*
  8vo.

JOHN HENRY HOBART, D. D., Bishop of the
  P. E. Church in the State of New York.
  HALF LENGTH, in robes. J. PARADISE, *Pinxt* 8vo.

ELIAS BOUDINOT. HALF LENGTH. WALDO AND
  JEWETT, *Pinxt.* 8vo.

G. PARKER,

AN Engraver in the stipple manner, was
an Englishman by birth, but at what time
he came to this country, and where he acquired the art, could not be ascertained.

He engraved a number of plates for "The National Portrait Gallery," and was regularly employed by the Book Publishers of the day. He died in New York about the year 1868.

DAVID HUMPHREYS, LL. D. HALF LENGTH, sitting at a table, both hands resting upon an upright book. G. STUART, *Pinxt.* 8vo.

NOAH WEBSTER. HALF LENGTH, sitting. JAS. HERRING, *Pinxt.* 8vo.

WILLIAM BAINBRIDGE, U. S. N. HALF LENGTH. J. W. JARVIS, *Pinxt.* 8vo.

ROBERT FULTON. THREE QUARTER LENGTH, sitting. B. WEST, P. R. A., *Pinxt.* 8vo.

JOSEPH STORY, LL. D. HALF LENGTH. CHESTER HARDING, *Pinxt.* 8vo.

MAHLON DICKERSON. HALF LENGTH. J. VANDERLYN, *Pinxt.* 8vo.

MAJOR GENERAL THOMAS SUMTER. HALF LENGTH, in uniform. C. W. PEALE, *Pinxt.* 8vo.

EDWARD EVERETT. FULL BUST, showing right hand, a cloak thrown over the breast and shoulders. A. B. DURAND, *Pinxt.* 8vo.

PROSPER M. WETMORE. HALF LENGTH. H. INMAN, N. A., *Pinxt.* 8vo.

CHARLES WILSON PEALE

WAS born of English parents at Chestertown, on the Eastern shore of Maryland, April 16, 1741. At the age of twenty-one, having served his time with a saddler of Annapolis (then the metropolis of the State), he commenced for himself, combining with his trade several others, such as coach-making, and clock and watch-making, besides working as a silversmith, and finally trying his hand at portrait painting. In the latter he had some little instruction from a Mr. Hesselius, an Englishman, who married and settled in Annapolis in the year 1763.

In 1768-9, he visited Boston, and was kindly received by J. S. Copley, then established as a portrait painter, who lent him a picture to copy. Upon his return to Annapolis he determined upon a voyage to London, and being assisted by several gentlemen of the former place, the loan to be returned with pictures, he sailed for England, arriving in London in 1770. Benjamin West received him into his house, and he studied during 1770-1, in the Royal Academy, under that painter's direction, at the same time turning his attention to modeling in wax, moulding and casting in plaster, painting in miniature, and engraving in Mezzotinto. On his return to Annapolis, he found constant employment as a portrait painter, and two years later established himself at Philadelphia.

Peale was a captain of volunteers, and was present at the battles of Trenton and Germantown, and while in camp painted the portraits of many officers, and he has the honorable distinction of being the painter of the first authentic portrait of

Washington (1772). He also represented Philadelphia in the State Legislature in 1777.

While prosecuting his art, he at the same time turned his attention to natural history, forming by his own efforts and the contributions of others, an exceedingly interesting collection, widely known, subsequently, in connection with his portraits of the prominent men of the time, as "Peale's Museum," the first in the country. In his efforts as a lecturer on Natural History, the loss of his front teeth interfering with his enunciation, he became a dentist to supply the deficiency, first working in ivory, and then making porcelain teeth for himself and others.

His trades, employments and professions may be summed up as follows : saddler and harness maker ; clock and watchmaker ; silversmith ; painter in oil, crayons and miniature; modeler in clay, wax and plaster, and engraver in Mezzotinto. He sawed the ivory for his miniatures, moulded the glasses and made the shagreen cases; he was a soldier, a legislator and a lecturer; a preserver of animals, whose deficiencies he supplied by means of glass eyes and artificial limbs, and a dentist; and to crown all was, in the words of his son, Rembrandt, "a mild, benevolent and good man."

He died at Philadelphia, Feb. 22, 1827.

The following prints are engraved in the Mezzotinto manner:

WILLIAM PITT, EARL OF CHATHAM. FULL FIGURE, in Roman classical costume, standing beside an altar to Liberty, bearing the inscription, "Sanctus Amor Patriæ Dat Animum." In the lower margin the words, "Worthy of Liberty, Mr. Pitt scorns to invade the Liberties of other People." CHARLES WILSON Peale, *Pinxt. et fecit.* Large folio.

G. WASHINGTON, Esq., late Commander-in-Chief of the Armies of the United States of America.

HEAD AND BUST, three quarter face. Painted and Engraved by C. W. PEALE, 1787. 4to. Oval.

THE MARQUIS DE LA FAYETTE, Major-General in the Armies of the United States of America. HEAD AND BUST, full face. C. W. PEALE, *Pinxt. et fecit.* 4to. Oval.

BENJ. FRANKLIN. HEAD AND BUST, three quarter face, wearing spectacles. C. W. PEALE, *Pinxt. et fecit.* 4to. Oval.

THE REVEREND JOSEPH PILMORE, Rector of the United Churches of Trinity, St. Thomas and All-Saints. HEAD AND BUST, in robes. Painted and Engraved by C. W. PEALE, 1787. 4to. Oval.

JOSEPH IVES PEASE,

LINE ENGRAVER, was born at Norfolk, Conn., August 9, 1809. At the age of fourteen he was placed in a dry goods store in Hartford, and employed his leisure hours in imitating such drawings and engravings as came under his notice. He soon, however, discovered that trade would not suit him, and returned home. His first attempts at engraving were made with an old awl for a tool, and a bit of thermometer brass for a plate, the impressions being worked off on a roll press of his own construction.

His parents, removing to Hartford, he was placed with Oliver Pelton, engraver, of that place, with whom he remained until of age, Pelton in the meantime having removed his establishment to Boston. About the year 1835 he went to Philadelphia, where he was kept constantly employed by the different publishers of that city. In 1848 he went to Stockbridge, Mass., and finally settled on a farm, "Twin Lakes," Salisbury, Conn.

Of late years Mr. Pease has been entirely engaged on Bank Note work. His plates mostly for Books are engraved with much taste and excellence of execution, and are faithful translations of the originals.

WASHINGTON AND HARVEY BIRCH. A. B. DURAND, *Pinxt.* 8vo.

THE DISAGREEABLE SURPRISE. W. S. MOUNT, *Pinxt.* 8vo.

RUSTIC CIVILITY. W. COLLINS, *Pinxt.* 8vo.

THE GHOST BOOK. G. H. COMEGYS, *Pinxt.* 8vo.

THE MILITIA TRAINING. J. G. CLONNEY, *Pinxt.* 8vo.

SUMMER, Mumble the Peg. H. INMAN, *Pinxt.* 8vo.

WINTER SPORT, The Rabbit Trap. W. S. MOUNT, *Pinxt.* 8vo.

THE TOUGH STORY. W. S. MOUNT, *Pinxt.* 8vo.

THE YOUNG TRADERS. W. PAGE, *Pinxt.* 8vo.

OLD '76 AND YOUNG '48, R. C. WOODVILLE, *Pinxt.* Ob. 4to. Am. Art Union Print, 1851.

THE LAST SUPPER. Copy of RAPHAEL MORGHEN'S Print.

HAINES FALLS, CATTSKILL MOUNTAINS.

OLIVER PELTON,

ENGRAVER in the line and stipple manner, was born at Portland, Conn., August 15, 1799, and when about seventeen years of age, entered with Abner Read, a bank-note engraver, of Hartford, to learn the art.

Mr. Pelton worked assiduously to acquire a knowledge of engraving, applying himself to executing vignettes, the most difficult part of the business, and after two years of constant effort was taken into partnership by Mr. Read and a certain Samuel Stiles. For some years they did a large business, his partners finally retiring, leaving him to prosecute it alone.

Samuel G. Goodrich (Peter Parley), one of his earliest patrons, removing to Boston in 1827, for the purpose of publishing a series of annals, which required the services of a number of engravers, induced Mr. Pelton to accompany him. The enterprise succeeded, and was continued for some ten years, during which time he was kept constantly employed.

In the year 1836 Mr. Pelton formed a partnership with Wm. D. Terry for bank note engraving, which was finally merged into the New England Bank Note Co. of Boston.

In 1850, he engraved a series of Portraits of the Poets for the publications of Phillips, Sampson and Co., of Boston. He has also engraved a large plate of "The Last Supper" for the New York "Evangelist," used by them as a premium.

Mr. Pelton removed to Hartford in 1860, and since that time has engraved a large number of Bible Plates, Portraits, &c.

WILLIAM HENRY HARRISON. HALF LENGTH. A. G. HOYT, *Pinxt.* 1840. Engraved in conjuction with D. Kimberly. Pub. at Boston, 1841. Folio.

EDWARD EVERETT. HALF LENGTH. Up. oval. 8vo.

JACOB PERKINS.

THIS ingenious mechanic and inventor was born in Newburyport, Mass., July 9th, 1766. He was apprenticed to a goldsmith of his native place, and distinguished himself quite early in life by the invention of a new method of plating shoe-buckles, then universally worn, and in the manufacture of which he engaged with considerable success.

When about twenty-one years of age he was employed by the Commonwealth of Massachusetts to make dies for copper coinage, and soon afterwards invented a machine for cutting and heading nails at one operation.

Early in the present century Mr. Perkins became interested in the production of Bank Note Plates, but soon discovering that the expense attending the engraving of the Note on a single plate, and the limited number of impressions afforded from copper, interfered seriously with the business, substituted steel for the softer metal, and originated the process of transferring engravings from one plate to another.

Previous to this time (1808) steel had been used for engraving, but in one instance in England (1805), in the production of a plate for "Smith's Topographical Illustrations of Westminster."

In the use of steel for engraving, where the transfer is intended to be made, the subject is first engraved on a small piece of the metal, which is then hardened and known by the technical term of die-plate. A decarbonized cylinder, large enough to receive the impression, is then rolled over it by means of a powerful machine, termed the transfer press, until the engraved work appears upon it in relief. The cylinder, or roll, in its turn is hardened, after which it is used in the same press for reproducing any number of fac-similes of the original die-plate, each of which will be an exact counterpart of the original.

In Bank Note work, which is the most

important application of this process, and
to which it owes its origin, the vignettes,
portraits, and other portions of the note are
engraved on small, separate, single plates,
or dies, as above-mentioned, and then trans-
ferred by the different rolls, to one large
plate, in such manner as to make up the
whole note to be printed from.

This transfer process, in connection with
the application of lathe work to the die-
plate, has given, in gradual improvements,
most marked, perhaps, in the perfection of
the geometrical lathe, so great a superiority
to the Bank Note plates of this country,
over those of all others, as to fully entitle
this branch of engraving to be termed an
American art.

Steel plates for picture engraving came
to be used about the year 1820, and in consequence of their superiority over copper,
as regards the greater number of impres-

sions to be obtained, have gradually taken place of, and almost entirely superseded the use of the latter metal.

About the year 1814, Perkins went to Philadelphia, and became associated with the firm of Murray, Draper, Fairman & Co., of that city, Bank Note engravers, with whom he remained several years, still experimenting upon and improving his machinery. It was while he was in Philadelphia that Asa Spencer, another Eastern man of great ingenuity, also connected with the same firm, invented the method of applying lathe work for the counters of Bank Notes.

This adaptation of the geometric lathe, although but a new application of an old principle, was made so successfully, that Spencer is entitled to as much credit for it as if he had been the original inventor.

In the year 1818, Perkins, accompanied by Gideon Fairman, Asa Spencer, and a number of workmen, went to London to compete for the premium of £20,000 offered by the Bank of England for a Bank Note which could not be counterfeited.

The superiority of their work was immediately recognized, but an English engraver having succeeded, after many efforts, in making a copy of the lathe work, they were obliged to withdraw from the contest. The Bank Directors, however, be it said to their credit, allowed them the sum of £5,000, in consideration of their ingenuity, and the trouble and expense they had gone to in the matter.

While in England they became connected with Charles Heath, the engraver, Perkins' and Fairman's names appearing with his on some book plates published about 1820, '22, marked as being engraved on "Patent Hardened Steel Plates."

Fairman and Spencer returned to this

country, but Perkins retained his connection with Mr. Heath, having obtained the privilege of supplying the Bank of Ireland with Bank-note plates.

Jacob Perkins died at London, July 30, 1849.

ROBERT PIGGOT, D. D.,

An engraver in the Stipple manner, was born in New York in the year 1795, and is of English descent. An early inclination to drawing, determined him to study engraving, and for that purpose he went to Philadelphia and became a student under David Edwin.

When scarcely of age he entered into a business arrangement with a fellow-pupil, Charles Goodman, with whom he was associated for several years, all the prints enumerated below bearing both their names as engravers.

Although quite an enthusiast in his love of art, and displaying considerable talent, and rapidly coming into notice, he soon abandoned the profession, studied divinity, and was ordained a minister of the Protestant Episcopal Church, in which sphere of duty he has ever since zealously labored. He resides in Baltimore County, Maryland.

JAMES MONROE, L.L. D., **President of the United States.** FULL LENGTH, sitting, holding a paper in his left hand, the right arm resting easily on the arm of the chair. In the left distance through some architecture may be seen the Capitol Buildings. C. B. KING, *Pinxt.* Roy. folio. Published Dec. 15, 1817, by W. H. Morgan, No. 114 Chesnut St., Philada.

G. H. E. MUHLENBERG, Th. D. und Prediger in Lancaster; geb. den 17ten Nov. 1753, starb den 23ten Mai, 1815; Seines Alters 61 Jahr, 6 M., 6T. FULL BUST. C. W. PEALE, *Pinxt.* 8vo.

REVD. JOSEPH PILMORE, D. D. FULL BUST, in robes. J. NEAGLE, *Pinxt.* 4to. Pub. 1819.

REV. JOHN WESLEY, A. M., late Fellow of Lincoln College, Oxford, and Founder of the Methodist Church. FULL BUST, in robes, in the act of speaking. Folio.

CASPAR WISTAR, M. D, FULL BUST.   8vo.

N. CHAPMAN, M. D., **Professor of the Institutes and Practice of Medicine and Clinical Practice in the University of Pennsylvania.** HALF LENGTH, in the act of speaking. T. SULLY, *Pinxt.* 8vo.

J. S. DORSEY, M. D. HALF LENGTH, sitting, both hands lying on a Book, T. SULLY, *Pinxt.* 8vo.

PEYTON RANDOLPH. FULL BUST. C. W. PEALE, *Pinxt.* 8vo.

A. J. DALLAS, Esq. FULL BUST. G. STUART, *Pinxt.* 8vo.

JAMES A. BAYARD, Esq. FULL BUST. WERTMULLER, *Pinxt.* 8vo.

WILLIAM LEWIS, Esq. HALF LENGTH, sitting. G. STUART, *Pinxt.* 8vo.

J. F. E. PRUD'HOMME,

AN engraver in the Stipple manner, was born on the island of St. Thomas (of French parents) the fourth day of October, 1800. The family came to this country about the year 1807, and settled in the city of New York in the Spring of 1809.

When about fourteen years of age he turned his attention to engraving, having for preceptor his brother-in-law, Thomas Gimbrede, but who, shortly afterwards, accepting the situation of Teacher of Drawing at West Point, left the subject of our notice to pursue his own course in life. He commenced as a portrait engraver, but finding little encouragement was forced to practice the art in a general way, which he continued for some years. At the instance of James Herring, who was about starting (1831) "The National Portrait Gallery of Distinguished Americans," he was induced to resume portrait engraving, and executed for that work several plates.

In the year 1852, he entered a bank note engraving establishment, and is now employed as an ornamental designer and engraver in the Treasury Department at Washington City.

He is a good draughtsman and an excellent engraver.

"Friar Puck" and "The Velvet Hat," are beautiful examples of the art.

BRIG. GEN. ANTHONY WAYNE. HALF LENGTH, in uniform. J. TRUMBULL, *Delt.* 8vo.

MAJ. GEN. HENRY KNOX. HALF LENGTH, in uniform, standing, his left hand on the muzzle of a cannon. G. STUART, *Pinxt.* 8vo.

BRIG. GEN. DANIEL MORGAN. HALF LENGTH, in the dress of a Virginia rifleman, (a loose coat ornamented with fringe.) J. TRUMBULL, *Delt.* 8vo.

JOHN EAGER HOWARD. HALF LENGTH. CHESTER HARDING, *Pinxt.* 8vo.

PETER GANSEVOORT. HALF LENGTH, in uniform. G. STUART, *Pinxt.* 8vo.

Mrs. D. P. MADISON. HALF LENGTH. J. WOOD, *Pinxt.* 8vo.

WINFIELD SCOTT. HEAD AND FULL BUST. R. W. WEIR, *Pinxt.* 8vo.

FRIAR PUCK. A CHILD, in a Friar's gown and hood. J. G. CHAPMAN, *Pinxt.* 8vo.

THE VELVET HAT. JAS. INSKEEP, *Delt.* 8vo.

THE DECLARATION OF INDEPENDENCE. Painted by JOHN TRUMBULL, ESQ. Ob. folio.

PAUL REVERE,

THE Patriot of 1775, was born at Boston, January 1, 1735, where he died the Tenth day of May, 1818. His father, of Hugenot descent, was a goldsmith by trade, and brought up his son to the same profession.

In 1756 he was a lieutenant of artillery, and was stationed at Fort Edward, near Lake George. On his return he established himself as a goldsmith, and began to acquire the art of engraving, in which he was entirely self-taught. He engraved the plates, made the press, and printed the Bills for the Continental notes, the first of which were issued in 1775.

His connection with the destruction of the tea in Boston Harbor, his celebrated ride on the night of April 18, 1775, to give notice of the British Expedition to Concord, and the many valuable services rendered to his country during our revolutionary struggle, have made his name prominent in its annals as that of an earnest, zealous patriot.

PORTRAIT OF JONATHAN MAYHEW, D. D.

THE REPEAL OF THE STAMP ACT. An emblematic print. Engraved in 1776.

THE SEVENTEEN RESCINDERS. A caricature print.

THE BLOODY MASSACRE, perpetrated in King Street, Boston, on March 5, 1770, by a party of the 29th Regt. Pub. 1770. "Engraved, printed and sold by Paul Revere, Boston."

THE LANDING of the British Troops in Boston. Engraved in 1774.

JAMES R. RICE,

LINE and stipple engraver, was born at Syracuse, N. Y., in 1824, and studied the art under his brother, W. W. Rice, in the office of Rawdon, Wright, Hatch & Co., Bank-note Engravers, of New York city.

He has been principally employed on Book work, Bible Illustrations, and the like, all of which are executed in line. Mr. Rice has resided in Philadelphia since 1851. The following prints are well engraved in the mixed manner.

T. S. ARTHUR. HEAD AND BUST. S. J. FERRIS, *Delt.* Folio.

THE GUARDIAN ANGEL. JOS. JOHN, *Pinxt.* Roy. Folio.

I KNOW THAT MY REDEEMER LIVETH. JOS. JOHN, *Pinxt.* Roy. folio,

A. H. RITCHIE.

Of this admirable engraver in the mezzotinto manner no certain particulars can be given, that artist having declined furnishing any.

He is said to be a Scotchman by birth, but to have acquired the art in this country, turning his attention to it about thirty years ago. He is a resident of Brooklyn, N. Y., and is about sixty-five years of age.

His last important Plate, the "Death of Lincoln," engraved from his own painting, a fine, effective composition, and excellently executed, presents a perfect fac-simile of the Room in which that event transpired, and comprises Twenty-six full-length portraits of those who were actually gathered around the couch of the dying President on the night of April 14, 1865.

GEORGE WASHINGTON. FULL LENGTH, Standing left hand, resting on a dress sword. P. F. ROTHERMEL, *Pinxt.* Pub. N. Y., 1852. Imp. folio.

S. VAN RENSELEAR. HEAD AND FULL BUST. C. HARDING, *Pinxt.* 4to.

AMOS KENDALL, of the District of Columbia. HEAD AND FULL BUST. 8vo.

MERCY'S DREAM. D. HUNTINGTON, *Pinxt.* Imp. folio. Art Union of Philadelphia, 1850.

WASHINGTON AND HIS GENERALS. Drawn and Engraved by A. H. RITCHIE. Ob. imp. folio.

LADY WASHINGTON'S RECEPTION DAY. D. HUNTINGTON, *Pinxt.* Ob. imp. folio.

ON THE MARCH TO THE SEA. F. O. C. DARLEY, *Delt.* Extra imp. folio. *Mixed.* This Plate was destroyed after taking 2,323 impressions.

DEATH OF LINCOLN. A. H. RITCHIE, *Pinxt.* Ob. imp., folio.

WILLIAM ROLLINSON,

A NATIVE of England, was born in the year 1760. His original business was that of chaser of fancy buttons, and he came to New York with a view of pursuing it in this country. Not long after his arrival General Knox, First Secretary of War under the Federal Government, employed him to chase the arms of the United States upon a set of gilt buttons for the coat which was worn by General Washington on the day of his inauguration as President.

Rollinson would not receive any compensation for this, declaring that he was more than paid by having the honor of working for such a man and for such an occasion. He was employed by silver-smiths until 1791, when he made his first attempt at plate engraving without any previous knowledge of the art, the essay being a small profile portrait of Gen. Washington, done in the stipple manner.

He engraved several plates for Brown's Family Bible, published in New York by Hodge, Allen and Campbell, and found employment with the Book Publishers of the day. Among the portraits executed by him is one of Alexander Hamilton after Archibald Robertson, and another of James Lawrence, U. S. N., after G. Stuart.

In 1812 Mr. Rollinson invented a machine to rule waved lines for engraving margins to Bank Notes, and in connection with W. S. Leney produced a specimen note which was favorably received, and induced many orders from different parts of the United States. In the seventieth year

10

of his age he executed a vignette for an edition of Horace by Professor Anthon.

He was living in 1834, the seventy-fourth year of his age, continuing to work " with unabated ardor and improved skill." (Dunlap, Hist. of the Arts of Design in the U. S.)

CHARLES BALTHAZAR JULIEN FEVRET DE SAINT MEMIN

WAS born at Dijon, France, on the 12th day of March, 1770, and quite early in life showed an aptitude for design, and displayed considerable mechanical talent.

Destined for the profession of arms, he entered as a cadet at the military school in Paris, April 1, 1784, was appointed supernumerary ensign in the following year, and ensign April 27, 1788. His sympathies at the outbreak of the French revolution, were with the Royal family, and the army of the princes being formed, he joined it, and served in that organization until it was disbanded, at which time he was entitled to the rank of lieutenant colonel, which was afterwards (Jan. 29, 1817,) conferred upon him by Louis XVIII., taking grade from May 1, 1792. While with the army, he turned his attention, during his leisure hours, to drawing and painting.

He came to America from Switzerland, where he had learned to gild and carve in wood, landing in Canada in 1793, and from thence going to New York, in which city he learned to engrave.

Towards the end of the last century, a French engraver named Queneday had invented a machine, by means of which he copied the human profile mathematically accurate. The outline alone was thus ob-

tained for the copper in a continuous line,
and the artist shaded and worked out the
interior detail with sufficient skill to give a
certain appearance of truth to the physiog-
nomy.   This invention, termed *physiono-
tracy*, had great success.

Saint Memin, knowing of the popularity
of this process, practiced after the death of
Queneday by Chretien and others, determined to introduce it into this country,
and therefore applied himself to the making of such a machine, according to his
own understanding of it, and also made a
pantograph.

His profiles were produced of life size
by the physionotrace, and finished in crayon,
the pantograph reducing them to the size
required for the plate, the portrait being
drawn in a perfect circle of a little more
than two inches in diameter.   Having thus
obtained the perfect outline, the details

were worked up by the graver, the shading being finished with the roulette, the latter tool being made by a machine of his own invention.

These profile portraits produced very rapidly, number about eight hundred, and are interesting, most of them being likenesses of the prominent personages of the time.

He worked in the prosecution of this portrait-making at New York, Philadelphia, Washington, and other prominent cities of the Union, until the year 1800, when he made a visit to his native country, of two years' duration. Upon his return he abandoned engraving for portrait and landscape painting. In the latter part of 1814, he returned to France finally, and at the time of his decease, which occurred June 23, 1852, was Director of the Museum at Dijon, to which office he had been appointed July 27, 1817.

JOHN SARTAIN,

ONE of the best engravers in the mezzo-tinto manner now working in America, is a native of the city of London, born in the year 1808.

Manifesting at an early age a strong proclivity for art, he was placed with an engraver to learn the general branches of the profession. When but fifteen, he had made sufficient advancement in drawing, as well as in the use of the graver, to attract the attention of William Young Ottley, the eminent writer on art, under whose direction Mr. Sartain was employed for two years on plates for his work, known as the "Italian School of Design," executed in line.

Early in the year 1828 his attention was attracted towards mezzo-tinto as a much more effective and expeditious method.

In 1830 he came to this country, and through the persuasion of the late Thomas Sully, settled in Philadelphia, but not finding immediate occupation in engraving, practiced portrait painting.

In 1842–43 he was proprietor and editor of Campbell's semi-monthly magazine, and during the latter portion of the time also editor of Sartain's Union Magazine.

Mr. Sartain, the first in America to engrave to any extent in mezzo-tinto, possesses great energy and perseverance, and it may be said that he has produced more works than any other living engraver. "Christ Rejected," after Benjamin West, and "The Iron Worker and King Solomon," after C. Schussele, the largest and most important mezzo-tinto Plates as yet executed in this country are admirably engraved, and his Portraits of Sir Thomas Lawrence, Robert Gilmore, and Professor

James J. Mapes, the latter from his own drawing, are very fine examples of the art.

He has always taken great interest in art matters, and his services as a member of and Secretary to the Board of Directors of "The Pennsylvania Academy of the Fine Arts" are well known and appreciated by those connected with that Institution.

He is now engaged upon a large plate, "The Battle of Gettysburg," after Peter F. Rothermel's admirable picture.

WILLIAM PENN. Full Length. H. Inman, *Pinxt.* Folio.

HENRY CLAY. Full Length in the act of speaking. John Neagle, *Pinxt.* Pub. 1843. Folio.

MARTIN VAN BUREN. Full Length. H. Inman, *Pinxt.* Folio.

SIR THOS. LAWRENCE. Scipe, *Pinxt.* Folio.

ROBERT GILMORE. Sir Thos. Lawrence, *Pinxt.* Folio.

MRS. ROBERT GILMORE. Sir Thos. Lawrence, *Pinxt.* Folio.

PROFESSOR JAMES J. MAPES. J. Sartain, *Delt.* 4to.

ADAM AND EVE. Copy of Marc Antonio's celebrated Print. 4to.

CHRIST REJECTED. Benj. West, *Pinxt.* Ob. Imp. Folio.

THE IRON WORKER AND KING SOLOMON. C. Schussele, *Pinxt.* Ob. Imp. folio.

ZEISBERGER PREACHING TO THE INDIANS. C. Schussele, *Pinxt.* Ob. Imp. folio.

MEN OF PROGRESS. C. Schussele, *Pinxt.* Ob. Imp. folio.

COUNTY ELECTION IN MISSOURI, G. C. Bingham, *Pinxt.* Ob. Imp. folio.

HOME ON FURLOUGH. C. Schussele, *Delt.* Pub. 1864. Ob. folio.

EUGENIE, Empress of France and Ladies of her Court. Winterhalter, *Pinxt.* Ob. 4to.

THE RETURN FROM MARKET. J. L. Krimmel, *Pinxt.* Ob. folio·

THE VALLEY OF THE BATTENKILL. Boutelle, *Pinxt.* Ob. folio.

SAMUEL SARTAIN,

Son of John Sartain, was born at Philadelphia, in October, 1830. He began the study of art in his fifteenth year, and rapidly

acquired skill as an engraver in the mixed
style, under the instruction of his father.
At the age of sixteen he executed an
excellent portrait of Benjamin West, after
Harlow.

He has produced considerable work in
pure line, his last in this style being the
pictorial embellishments to the Certificate
of Stock for "The Pennsylvania Academy
of the Fine Arts," the entire design for
which is from his pencil.

Of the large number of plates executed
by him we select the following.

Dr. **PHILIP S. PHYSICK.**   H. INMAN, *Pinxt.*   8vo.

LIEUT. THOS. BIDDLE.   T. SULLY, *Pinxt.*   8vo.

SAMUEL COATES.   T. SULLY, *Pinxt.*   8vo.

JUDGE JOHN M. READ.   J. HENRY BROWN, *Pinxt.*
     8vo.

JOHN HARE POWEL.   SIR THOS. LAWRENCE, *Pinxt.*
     8vo.

Rev. **D. P. F. MAYER.**   J. NEAGLE, *Pinxt.*   Folio.

CHIEF JUSTICE TANEY.   F. B. MAYER, *Pinxt.*   4to.

ONE OF THE CHOSEN. S. J. Guy, *Pinxt.* 4to.

CLEAR THE TRACK. C. Schussele, *Pinxt.* Art Union of Philadelphia, 1854. Imp. folio.

THE SONG OF THE ANGELS. T. Moran, *Pinxt.* Folio.

EDWARD SAVAGE,

Painter and Engraver, in the mezzotinto and stipple manner, was born at Princetown, Mass., in the year 1761, and died there in July, 1817. His original calling was that of a goldsmith, which, however, he relinquished for portrait painting and engraving.

About the year 1792, he went abroad and studied in London for a time under Benjamin West, and afterwards visited Italy. He was a man of some talent, although his portraits are not remarkable as "counterfeit presentments," and in his plates he is said to have been materially aided by David Edwin and J. W. Jarvis.

GENERAL GEORGE WASHINGTON. HEAD AND BUST, in Uniform. Painted and engraved by E. SAVAGE. Up. oval in a rectangle. 8vo. *Stipple.*

GEORGE WASHINGTON, Esq., President of the United States of America. THREE-QUARTER LENGTH. Sitting with crossed legs; a chart spread over the right knee and partly on a table, is held by the right hand. E. SAVAGE, *Pinxt. et Sculp.* "From the original port., painted at the request of the Corporation of the University of Cambridge, Mass." Pub. June 25, 1793, by E. Savage, No. 54 Newman Street. Folio. *Mezzotinto.*

DAVID RITTENHOUSE, LL. D., F. R. S., President of the Philosophical Society. HALF LENGTH. Sitting at a table on which are papers and a philosophical apparatus. C. W. PEALE, *Pinxt.* Pub. Philadelphia, Dec. 10, 1796, by E. Savage. Folio. *Mezzotinto.*

BENJAMIN FRANKLIN, LL. D., F. R. S. HALF LENGTH. Sitting at a table perusing a manuscript. The thumb of the right hand supports his chin. D. MARTIN, *Pinxt.* Folio. *Mezzotinto.*

THE WASHINGTON FAMILY. The title also in French. Painted and engraved by E. SAVAGE. "Philadelphia, Published March 10, 1798, by E. Savage and Robt. Wilkinson, No. 58 Cornhill, London." Ob. Roy. folio. *Stipple.*

STEPHEN A. SCHOFF.

THIS admirable line engraver was born at Danville, Vermont, January 16th, 1818.

He began engraving under the direction of Oliver Pelton, of Boston, with whom he remained until nearly of age, subsequently passing a short time with Joseph Andrews. In 1840, in company with the latter, he visited Europe, and spent about two years in Paris studying drawing and perfecting himself in the art. Mr. Schoff has given most of his time and attention to bank-note work. His portraits and vignettes are among the very best produced; the female heads, for delicacy, taste and excellence of execution, being almost unequalled in this branch of the art.

The portrait of William Penn mentioned below, is carefully and skilfully engraved.

WILLIAM PENN. October 14, 1666. Ætat. 22. *Pax Quæritur Bello.* HEAD AND FULL BUST, in armor, the hair worn long. From a portrait by an unknown artist, presented to the Historical Society of Penna. by his grand-son, Granville Penn. Folio.

JARED SPARKS. HALF LENGTH. T. SULLY, *Pinxt.* 8vo.

A. HUMBOLDT. Head and Bust. M. Wight, *Pinxt.* 4to.

SAMUEL APPLETON. Head and Bust. G. P. A. Healy. *Pinxt.* 4to.

WILLIAM CULLEN BRYANT. Head and Full Bust. Up. oval in a rectangle. A. B. Durand, *Pinxt.* Folio. Engraved in conjunction with Alfred Jones. Pub. by "The Century," 1858.

CAIUS MARIUS on the Ruins of Carthage. J. Vanderlyn, *Pinxt.* Folio.

ON THE PEMIGEWASSETT. (At West Campton, N. H.). Geo. L. Brown, *Pinxt.* Ob. folio.

SAMUEL SEYMOUR,

Line Engraver, an Englishman by birth, who practiced his art at Philadelphia in the first quarter of the present century. He was an excellent draughtsman, and in that capacity went with the expedition to the Yellow Stone River (1823-24), under Capt. Stephen H. Long.

He engraved quite a number of Book plates, including several for Rees' Cyclopædia.

THE U. S. FRIGATE UNITED STATES, Stephen Decatur, Esq., Commander, capturing his Britannic Majesty's Frigate Macedonian, John S. Carden, Esq., Commander. T. BIRCH, *Pinxt.* Ob. Roy. folio.

THE CITY OF PHILADELPHIA, in the State of Pennsylvania, North America. THOS. BIRCH, *Delt.* Ob. folio.

SCHUYLKILL BRIDGE, High Street, Philadelphia. W. BIRCH, *Delt.* Ob. folio. Pub. by W. Birch, May, 1805.

JAMES SMILLIE,

LANDSCAPE ENGRAVER, was born in the city of Edinburgh on the twenty-third day of November, 1807. When about eleven years of age, he was indentured to James Johnston, Silver Engraver, of that place, who dying about ten months afterwards, young Smillie went for a short time with Edward Mitchell, a general picture Engraver, during which time, however, he only drew with pen and pencil.

In 1820 the family came to America and settled in Quebec, where his father and eldest brother started business as jewellers, and for whom he commenced working as a general engraver, lettering, &c., planishing his own copper and doing his own printing. Lord Dalhousie, then Governor of the Canadas, noticing his talent, gave him a free passage to London, with letters of introduction, which, however, proved an injury; for the engravers to whom he applied for instruction, regarding him as a protegé of the Governor, demanded excessive premiums. He was therefore obliged to abandon the idea of studying in London, and went to Edinburgh, and entered (1828) into an agreement with a certain Andrew Wilson, which lasted for five months, when he returned to Quebec.

In 1829 he went to New York city, where he has since lived,) his engraving

of "The Convent Gate," after a picture by
R. W. Weir, bringing him into notice. In
1834 he was elected associate of the National Academy of Design, and in 1851
Academician.

From the very first he has been inti-
mately connected with Bank-note engraving interests in this country, and to that
he now devotes all his time and attention.

James Smillie, conceded to be the best
landscape engraver in America, is altoge-
ther a self-educated man, overcoming every
obstacle by patient, persistent effort. His
plates, the most important in this particular
branch of the art yet produced in this
country, executed with great taste and
ability, are replete with fine artistic feeling,
and are truthful translations of the originals.

The well-known series of "The Voyage
of Life," after Thomas Cole, and "The

11

Rocky Mountains," after A. Bierstadt, are splendid examples of the art, quite equal to any contemporary European productions of a similar character.

THE CONVENT GATE. R. W. WEIR, *Pinxt.* 8vo.

BAY AND HARBOR OF NEW YORK, from Bedlow's Island. JOHN G. CHAPMAN, *Pinxt.* Ob. 4to. Pub. 1835.

DOVER PLAINS. A. B. DURAND, *Pinxt.* Ob. 4to. Am. Art Union Print, 1850.

MY OWN GREEN FOREST LAND. A. B. DURAND, P. N. A. D., *Pinxt.* 4to.

A WESTERN LAKE BY SUNSET. A. B. DURAND, *Pinxt.* 4to.

EVENING. A Scene in the Highlands, N. Y. R. W. WEIR, *Pinxt.* 4to.

THE BATTLE-FIELD OF BRANDYWINE. THOS. DOUGHTY, *Pinxt.* Ob. 4to.

DREAM OF ARCADIA. THOS. COLE, *Pinxt.* Ob. 4to. Am. Art Union Print, 1850.

MOUNT WASHINGTON, from the Valley of Conway. JOHN F. KENSETT, *Pinxt.* Ob. 4to. Am. Art Union Print, 1851.

AMERICAN HARVESTING, JASPER F. CROPSEY, *Pinxt.* Ob. 4to. Am. Art Union Publication, 1851.

THE LAND OF THE CYPRESS. D. Huntington, *Pinxt.* Ob. 8vo.

THE VOYAGE OF LIFE. A Series of Four.
  Childhood.
  Youth.
  Manhood.
  Old Age.
Thos. Cole, *Pinxt.* Ob. Roy. folio. Pub. 1855.

THE ROCKY MOUNTAINS, Lander's Peak. Albert Bierstadt, *Pinxt.* Ob. imp. folio. Pub. 1866.

JAMES D. SMILLIE,

Line Engraver, son of James Smillie, was born in the city of New York, in 1833. His father instructed him in engraving, and even before he became of age, intrusted him with work of considerable importance.

He was chiefly employed on Bank-note work, until the year 1862, when, having terminated a three years' engagement with the American Bank Note Co., he visited Europe, and determined to become a

painter.   Two years subsequently, he took
a studio with his brother George, in New
York, and since that time has done very
little engraving, devoting himself to landscape painting.   His best productions are
the Illustrations for Cooper's Works, after
designs by F. O. C. Darley.

H. WRIGHT SMITH.

THIS excellent portrait engraver in the
stipple manner, born at Edinburgh, Scotland, in 1828, was brought to this country
when five years of age, the family settling
in New York City.

When about thirteen, he entered with
A. L. Dick of that place, to acquire the
art, remaining with him seven years, and
subsequently passed two years with Thomas Doney, an engraver, in the mezzotinto
manner.   He then (1850) removed to
Boston, and commenced practicing for

himself, returning to New York (where he now resides) about five years ago. His works, mostly for books, are quite numerous. We select the following as good examples, the Head of Washington, whether as an engraving or as a translation of the original, being equally meritorious, and the portraits of Charles Sumner and Wendell Phillips, fine in character, drawing and execution.

WASHINGTON. From the Head by STUART, in the Boston Athenæum. 4to.

DANIEL WEBSTER. FULL LENGTH. CHESTER HARDING, *Pinxt.* Roy. folio.

EDWARD EVERETT. THREE-QUARTER LENGTH. M. WRIGHT, *Pinxt.* Folio.

CHESTER HARDING. HALF LENGTH. *Se ipse*, *Pinxt.* Oval 4to.

RUFUS CHOATE. HEAD AND BUST. 8vo.

WENDELL PHILLIPS. HEAD AND BUST. 8vo.

CHARLES SUMNER. HEAD AND BUST. 8vo.

GEORGE TICKNOR. HEAD AND BUST. 8vo.

MARSHALL P. WILDER. HEAD AND BUST. Roy. 8vo.

SAMUEL BURNHAM. HEAD AND BUST. 8vo.

JAMES W. STEEL,

LINE ENGRAVER, was born at Philadelphia, in the year 1799. At sixteen years of age he entered with Benjamin Tanner to acquire the art, and with whom he remained until of age, during which time the Bank Note firm of Tanner, Vallance, Kearny & Co. was formed and dissolved. After becoming of age, he was employed by George Murray for about eighteen months.

Mr. Steel, at an advanced age, is still practicing at Bank Note work. The portrait of Commodore James Barron is well engraved, and is a good example of his abilities.

WASHINGTON IN 1772, Ætatis 40. THREE QUARTER LENGTH, in the costume of a Virginian Colonel. C. W. PEALE, *Pinxt.* 8vo.

COMMODORE JAMES BARRON, of the **U. S. Navy.** FULL BUST, in uniform, sword resting on right fore-arm. JOHN NEAGLE, *Pinxt.* Small 4to.

JOHN VAUGHAN, Esq. Full Bust, right hand resting on an upright folio vol. T. Sully, *Pinxt.* 8vo.

SAMUEL SLATER. Full Bust. In the lower margin a coat-of-arms, with the legend, "Crescit sub pondere virtus." Lincoln, *Delt.* 8vo.

REV. GREGORY T. BEDELL, D. D., Rector of St. Andrew's Church, Philadelphia. Full Bust, in robes, in the act of speaking. John Neagle, *Pinxt.* Large folio. Pub. 1831.

THE UNIVERSITY, (Philada.). Geo. Strickland, *Delt.* 8vo. "Childs' Views."

WIDOWS' AND ORPHANS' ASYLUM. " *Delt.* 8vo. "Childs' Views."

FRIENDS' MEETING HOUSE, MERION. Hugh Reinagle, *Pinxt.* 8vo. "Childs' Views."

BENJAMIN TANNER.

This excellent stipple and line engraver was born in the city of New York, March 27, 1775. At a very early age he displayed a talent for drawing and designing, and after receiving the best education afforded for youth in those days, entered the engraving and designing office of P. C. Verger, a Frenchman, where he remained until becoming of age.

In December, 1799, he went to Philadelphia to permanently establish himself, and soon became actively engaged in his profession, his brother, Henry S. Tanner, afterwards widely known as a map publisher, joining him in the year 1806, to whom he taught the geographical or map part of his business.

About the year 1816 he commenced, with others, a Bank-note Engraving Establishment, under the firm name of Tanner, Vallance, Kearny & Co., his brother Henry being the Co. The Bank-note co-partnership having expired by limitation, and his sight being seriously affected and his health impaired, he discontinued the finer branches of his profession, and in the year 1835 established a Stereographic Safety Blank Check, Note and Draft Publishing Office. This he continued until 1845, when he was attacked by an abscess of the brain, from

which he never rallied, and died at Baltimore, where he had been taken for better
care and attention, November 14, 1848.

G. WASHINGTON. HEAD AND BUST, in uniform.
SAVAGE, *Pinxt.* Up. oval. 8vo. *Stipple.*

JOHN ADAMS. HEAD AND FULL BUST. Small 4to.
Stipple.

**BENJAMIN FRANKLIN. Born at Boston, Jany.
17, 1706, died at Philadelphia, April 17, 1790.**
HEAD AND FULL BUST, wearing a fur cap. C. N.
COCHIN, *Pinxt.* 1777. 4to. Pub. 1822. *Stipple.*

**THE MOST REVEREND JOHN CARROLL,
D. D.** HALF LENGTH. Sitting in full robes. J. PAUL,
Pinxt. Engraved in conjunction with W. S. LENEY.
Roy. folio. Pub. 1812. *Stipple.*

REV. FRANCIS ASBURY. J. PARADISE, *Pinxt.*

APOTHEOSIS OF WASHINGTON. J. J. BARRALET,
Delt. Imp. folio. Pub. 1802. *Stipple.*

UNITED STATES AND MACEDONIA. T. BIRCH,
Pinxt. Ob. Roy. folio. Pub. 1813. *Line.*

**PERRY'S VICTORY on Lake Erie, Sept. 10,
1813.** J. J. BARRALET, *Delt.* Ob. Roy. folio. Pub.
1815. *Line.*

THE LAUNCH of the Steam Frigate FULTON.
J. J. BARRALET, *Delt.* Folio. Pub. 1815. *Line.*

MACDONOUGH'S VICTORY on Lake Champlain, and **DEFEAT** of the **British Army at Platts-burg, by General Macomb, Sept. 11, 1814.** H. Reinagle, *Pinxt.* Ob. Roy. folio. Pub. 1816. *Line.*

THE SURRENDER OF CORNWALLIS, at York-town. J. F. Renaulty, *Delt.* Ob. Roy. folio.

AMERICA GUIDED BY WISDOM. An allegorical representation of the U. S., denoting their Independence and Prosperity. J. J. Barralet, *Delt.* Ob. Roy. folio. *Line.*

CORNELIUS TIEBOUT,

An Engraver in the stipple manner, was born in New York about the year 1777. He began at quite an early age to exhibit a taste for drawing, and while an apprentice with J. Burger, (1790), a silversmith of that city, made some attempts at engraving on copper. In the year 1794 he engraved several heads for a work then being published by William Dunlap, "The German Theatre."

In 1795 he went to London to receive

regular instruction in the art, under James Heath, and returned very much improved, being the first American to visit London to study engraving. He chose Philadelphia as the place of his residence, and worked for the principal Book Publishers of that city.

After accumulating some property, he entered into certain speculations, which proving disastrous, he moved to the State of Kentucky, where he died. His plates are well-executed; the portrait of Gen. Gates is a fine example of his abilities as an engraver.

GEO. WASHINGTON. Head and Full Bust. G. Stuart, *Pinxt.* 8vo.

JOHN ADAMS. Half Length. Up. Oval. 4to.

THOMAS JEFFERSON. Head and Full Bust. G. Stuart, *Pinxt.* 8vo.

THOMAS JEFFERSON. Half Length. R. Peale, *Pinxt.* Up. Oval. 4to.

THOMAS JEFFERSON, President of the United States. Full Length, standing, holding in his right hand a paper which lies partly on a Table, entitled, "The Declaration of Independence." A Bust of Benj. Franklin and some Books on the Table. Peale, *Pinxt.* Roy. folio. Philada.

GENERAL GATES. Head and Full Bust, in uniform. G. Stuart, *Pinxt.* Up. Oval, folio. Pub. N. York. 1798.

COMMODORE TRUXTON, of the Navy of the U. S. Head and Bust, in uniform. A. Robertson, *Pinxt.* Up. Oval, folio. Pub. at Philada.

JOHN JAY, First Chief-Justice of the U. S. Head and Full Bust. G. Stuart, *Pinxt.* Folio. Pub. in London, 1795.

THE RIGHT REV. WILLIAM WHITE, D. D., Bishop of the Protestant Episcopal Church in the State of Penna. Half Length Sitting, in robes. S. Stuart, *Pinxt.* Folio.

THOMAS McKEAN, Governor of Pennsylvania. Head and Bust. Up. Oval. 4to. Pub. by D. Kennedy, No. 228 Market St.

SIMON SNYDER, Governor of Pennsylvania. Head and Bust in Profile. W. Woolley, *Pinxt.* Up. Oval. Folio.

VIEW OF THE WATER WORKS. at Centre Square, Philada. J. J. Barralet, *Delt.* Ob. folio.

WILLIAM E. TUCKER,

An excellent line engraver, a pupil of Francis Kearny, was born at Philadelphia in 1801, where he died in the year 1857.

His plates are well engraved, and in fine taste, particularly the border and flower work furnished for magazines. He was much employed on bank note work.

THE FARMER'S BOY. Shayer, *Pinxt.* 8vo.

WINTER SPORTS. Boys Coasting. J. G. Chapman, *Pinxt.* 8vo.

SPORTSMAN AND DOGS. T. Doughty, *Pinxt.* 8vo.

A DISTINGUISHED MEMBER OF THE HUMANE SOCIETY. A Newfoundland Dog, Head and Breast. After E. and T. Landseer. Oval, in an ornamented rectangle. 4to. *Mezzotinto.*

BANK OF PENNSYLVANIA, Philadelphia. G. Strickland, *Delt.* 8vo.

FAIRMOUNT WATERWORKS, Philadelphia, from the Reservoir. T. Doughty, *Pinxt.* 8vo.

PENNSYLVANIA HOSPITAL, Philadelphia, 1856, Pine St. Front. McArthur, *Delt.* 8vo.

PENNSYLVANIA HOSPITAL for the INSANE.
W. Mason, *Delt.* 4to.

P. C. VERGER,

Line Engraver, a Frenchman by birth, who practiced in New York toward the close of the last century, having at that time as a pupil, the well-known engraver, Benjamin Tanner.

His name appears as engraver on the following print :

TRIUMPH OF LIBERTY. An allegorical design, dedicated to its defenders in America. J. F. Renault, *Delt.*, N. Y., Sept., 1795. Ob. folio. Pub. N. Y., Nov., 1796.

ADAM B. WALTER,

Engraver in the mezzotinto and stipple manner, was born at Philadelphia in 1820, and died there on the fourteenth day of October last, 1875.

At fifteen years of age, he entered with Thomas B. Welch to learn the art of engraving, and at twenty was connected with him in business, their joint names appearing on many book illustrations. This connection lasted until 1848. He studied drawing under John Rubens Smith.

The plates mentioned below are well engraved.

GEORGE WASHINGTON, Patriæ Pater. HEAD AND BUST, in an oval, surrounded by an oak wreath, in a solidly engraved border representing stone-work, with a colossal Head as a Key-stone. Roy. folio. Copy of an original Lithograph by REMBRANDT PEALE, and of the same size.

MAJOR GEN. GEO. B. McCLELLAN, on the Battle-Field of Antietam. FULL FIGURE, on horseback. C. SCHUSSELE, *Pinxt.* Roy. folio. Pub. 1863.

WILLIAM WARNER,

AN Engraver in the Mezzotinto manner, in which he was entirely self-taught. He was a native of Philadelphia, had talent, and was a man of considerable ingenuity.

He died in the year 1848, being about thirty-five years of age.

GEN. WASHINGTON, on the Battle-Field at Trenton. Full Length, in uniform, a field-glass in his right hand. In the rear a horse held by an attendant. From the picture by John Trumbull, Yale College, New Haven. Roy. folio. Pub. 1845.

ALONZO POTTER, D. D., LL. D., Bishop of the P. E. Church, Penna. Full Length, standing in robes. W. E. Winner, *Pinxt.* Roy. folio.

The Honorable and Right REV. JOHN STRACHAN, D. D., Lord Bishop of Toronto. Half Length, sitting in robes. Berthin, *Pinxt.* Folio.

THOMAS B. WELCH.

This excellent engraver in the mezzotinto and stipple manner was born in Charleston, S. C., about the year 1814. In early life he was put to learning general engraving, and while acquiring the lettering branch, attracted the attention of a gentleman who urged him to follow the higher departments of the art. Accordingly, when about seventeen years of age, he went to Philadelphia and entered with Jas. B. Longacre, with whom he remained until of age.

He engraved many plates for the publications of the day, annuals, magazines, and the like, and frequently tried his hand at portrait painting. About the year 1861 he abandoned engraving, and went abroad for the purpose of practicing painting. He died at Paris, Nov. 5, 1874.

Welch was a good draughtsman, and engraved flesh extremely well. His head of Washington, after Stuart, is an admirable production, and among his small portraits those of Benjamin Franklin and Henry Laurens may be cited as fine examples of stipple engraving.

GEORGE WASHINGTON. From the head by STUART in the Boston Athenæum. Roy. folio.

JOHN ADAMS. HEAD AND FULL BUST. G. STUART. 8vo. *Mezzotinto.*

12

BENJAMIN FRANKLIN. HALF LENGTH, sitting at a Table reading a Manuscript. D. MARTIN, *Pinxt.* 8vo.

JAMES MADISON. HEAD AND FULL BUST, wearing a tight-fitting cap. J. B. LONGACRE, *Delt.* Montpelier, Va., July, 1833. 8vo.

HENRY LAURENS. HALF LENGTH, sitting in an arm-chair, inclining forward. J. S. COPLEY, *Pinxt.* 8vo.

ROBERT MORRIS. HALF LENGTH, sitting at a Table, inclining forward in a graceful manner, the left hand resting on a folio vol. which lies on the Table. R. E. PINE, *Pinxt.* 8vo.

THOMAS McKEAN. HALF LENGTH. On the left breast the order of the Cincinnati. G. STUART. *Pinxt.* 8vo.

GOV. STRONG, of Mass. HEAD AND FULL BUST. G. STUART, *Pinxt.* 8vo.

MAJOR GEN. WINFIELD SCOTT. HALF LENGTH, in uniform. Imp. folio.

FELIX GRUNDY. HALF LENGTH. W. B. COOPER, *Pinxt.* 8vo.

WILLIAM BARTRAM. HEAD AND FULL BUST. C. W. PEALE, *Pinxt.* 8vo.

NICHOLAS BIDDLE. HALF LENGTH SITTING, FULL FACE. REMBRANDT PEALE, *Pinxt.* Engraved in conjunction with J. B. Longacre. 8vo.

WILLIAM WHITE, D. D., Bishop P. E. Church of Pennsylvania, Ætat. 85. HEAD AND FULL BUST, in robes. 8vo.

REV. JOSEPH H. JONES, D. D. HALF LENGTH. Standing in a pulpit, both hands resting upon an open Bible. J. NEAGLE, *Pinxt.* 4to. *Mezzotinto.*

RIGHT REV. NATHANIEL BOWEN, D. D., Bishop of S. C. THREE-QUARTER LENGTH. Standing in robes, in the act of speaking, the left hand resting on a Bible. S. F. B. MORSE, *Pinxt.* 4to.

PHILIP TIDYMAN, D. D. Member of the American Philosophical Society, and of the Royal Society of Gottingen, etc. HALF LENGTH. THOS. SULLY, *Pinxt.* 4to.

E. WELLMORE,

AN Engraver in the stipple manner, who, during his minority, as a pupil of James B. Longacre, engraved, among others, the following portraits for "The National Portrait Gallery," that of Thomas Mifflin being the best.

He discontinued the art upon arriving at age, and studied for the ministry.

MAJOR GENERAL ARTHUR ST. CLAIR. HALF LENGTH, in uniform, in the right distance a view of an encampment. C. W. PEALE, *Pinxt.* 8vo.

MAJOR GENERAL CHARLES COTESWORTH PINCKNEY. HALF LENGTH, in uniform, showing right arm and hand. MALBONE, *Pinxt.* 8vo.

EDWARD SHIPPEN, LL.D. HEAD AND FULL BUST. G. STUART, *Pinxt.* 8vo.

THOMAS MIFFLIN. HEAD AND FULL BUST, in uniform. G. STUART, *Pinxt.* 8vo.

JAMES A. BAYARD. HEAD AND FULL BUST. WERTMULLER, *Pinxt.* 8vo.

MARTIN VAN BUREN. HALF LENGTH, sitting, left hand resting upon an upright book, on a table to the left. H. INMAN, *Pinxt.* 8vo.

WILLIAM WELLSTOOD.

THIS excellent line engraver was born at Edinburgh, Scotland, Dec. 19, 1819, and came to this country with his parents in May, 1830.

When about sixteen years of age, he began in the city of New York—where he still resides—as a letter engraver, gradually merging into the pictorial, attaining the art without other instruction than that afforded by close observation and persistent effort.

Mr. Wellstood has been much employed by the Western Methodist Book Concern of Cincinnati, which, by its publication of good engravings, has exercised a decided influence on public taste in that section of the country.

His plates, executed with much taste and ability, comprise portraits, subjects and landscapes, the latter branch of the art having received most of his attention.

From his numerous works the following are selected.

U. S. GRANT. Half Length. 4to.

HENRY W. LONGFELLOW. Full Length. A. Chappel, *Pinxt.* 4to.

FLORENCE NIGHTINGALE. Full Length. Roy. folio.

WALDEMERE. From a composition by C. F. Lessing. 4to.

NEW HAMPSHIRE SCENERY. R. W. Hubbard, *Pinxt.* Ob. 4to.

A QUIET NOOK. A. F. BELLOWS, *Pinxt.* Ob. 4to.

LIFE'S DAY A SERIES OF THREE. (4to and folio.) A. F. BELLOWS, *Pinxt.*
> *Morning.*—THE CHRISTENING.
> *Noon.*—THE WEDDING.
> *Night.*—THE BURIAL.

SUMMER, (In Maine.) A. D. SHATTUCK, *Pinxt.* Ob. 4to.

THE SUMMER TRESSES OF THE TREES ARE GONE. A. D. SHATTUCK, *Pinxt.* 4to.

ON THE COAST OF MT. DESERT. W. HART, *Pinxt.* Ob. 4to.

CHOCORUA PEAK. W. HART, *Pinxt.* Ob. 4to.

FRANCONIA NOTCH. S. R. GIFFORD, *Pinxt.* 4to.

MT. WASHINGTON. S. R. GIFFORD, *Pinxt.* Ob. 4to.

THE COMING STORM. D. JOHNSON, *Pinxt.* Ob. 4to.

ROBERT WHITECHURCH.

THIS excellent engraver in the line and stipple manner, was born in London, in the year 1814. When about thirty years of age, he turned his attention to engraving, and after a preparatory study of three years, came to America in 1848.

He settled in Philadelphia, and engaged with Thomas Illman, with whom he remained two years, and was afterwards employed by John M. Butler, Publisher, of that city. For the last ten years, he has been engaged on government work, residing in Philadelphia.

MAJOR GENERAL NATHANIEL GREENE. HEAD AND FULL BUST, in uniform. R. PEALE, *Pinxt*. 4to.

THOMAS MOORE. HEAD AND BUST. LAWRENCE, *Pinxt*. 8vo.

EDITH MAY. HEAD AND BUST. W. H. FURNESS, JR., *Pinxt*. 8vo.

U. S. SENATE, 1850. P. F. ROTHERMEL, *Delt*. Ob. Imp. folio. Pub. 1855.

FRANKLIN before the Lords in Council, Whitehall Chapel, London, 1774. C. SCHUSSELE, *Pinxt*. Ob. extra Imp. folio. Published by John M. Butler, Philada., 1859.

LINCOLN AND HIS CABINET. C. SCHUSSELE, *Pinxt*. Ob. Oval. 4to.

W. A. WILMER,

An Engraver in the stipple manner, a pupil of James B. Longacre. He resided in Philadelphia, and died about the year 1855, aged thirty-five years.

He engraved the following portraits for " The National Portrait Gallery."

JAMES MADISON. Half Length, sitting. G. Stuart, *Pinxt.*

SAMUEL JACKSON. (**Gov. of Geo., 1798-1801.**) Half Length, profile. After St. Memin.

MORDECAI GIST. (**Brig. Gen. U. S. A.**) Three Quarter Length, sitting in full uniform.

LUTHER MARTIN. (**Att'y Gen. of Md.**) Half Length.